Defiant Pose

Stewart Home

DEFIANT POSE

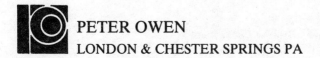 *A Novel*

PETER OWEN
LONDON & CHESTER SPRINGS PA

PETER OWEN PUBLISHERS
73 Kenway Road London SW5 0RE
Peter Owen books are distributed in the USA by
Dufour Editions Inc. Chester Springs PA 19425-0449

First published in Great Britain 1991
© Stewart Home 1989

British Library Cataloguing in Publication Data
Home, Stewart, *1962 –*
  Defiant Pose
  1. English Fiction
  I. Title
  823.914

  ISBN 0–7206–0828–7

Typesetting by Selectmove Ltd London W3
Printed in Great Britain by Billings of Worcester

One

Terry Blake didn't want to get involved in the conversations going on around him. His attention was half focused on a battered copy of Tony Parsons's *The Kids*. He read a paragraph, then eyed up the girl who'd parked her arse one seat down from where he was sitting. She looked about twenty-seven, was slim and her tits couldn't have been more than thirty-four. Terry decided that if nothing better turned up, he'd have her. So far there wasn't much competition, a couple of wimmin in their forties and a nineteen-year-old drenched in cheap perfume.

The blokes weren't much to look at either, a scruffy bunch of oddballs and misfits. Terry occasionally went for arses, but on the whole he preferred wimmin. The trouble with men, Terry reflected, was that they all wanted to stick their pricks into other people's holes. No man had ever known the skinhead, although he sometimes let a woman finger-fuck his arse. As far as Terry was concerned, the Ancient Greeks had a more progressive attitude towards gay sex than so-called modern civilization. They'd not looked down upon the active partner. Their warrior code had allowed the strong of either sex to prey upon those who did not possess the Will to Power.

With his neatly cropped hair, button-down shirt, sta-pres and Doctor Marten boots, Terry was the epitome of a working-class warrior. He prided himself on his smart and practical appearance. He was always ready for bother, geared up to battle the filthy hordes who threatened progressive socialist ideals with revisionist bullshit and even more upfront attempts to defend capitalist barbarism.

'I'm Kate Dobbs and I'm here to tell you about the EAS,' an old biddy announced as she marched into the room.

Terry checked his watch, the bitch was twenty minutes late. He'd got up early to come to the induction and once again he was being treated like shit. To the likes of Kate Dobbs he was no more than a social security number. Until a few weeks ago, Terry had been happily unemployed. His benefit and an undeclared income from a sideline in porno videos had supplied him with more than enough cash to meet his modest needs. Then some bureaucrat made him an offer he couldn't refuse. The government was going to help him find a job, and unless he gratefully accepted its assistance, his welfare would be cut.

Terry'd taken the easy option, he'd decided to go on the Enterprise Allowance Scheme. The government would pay him forty quid a week to run his own business. All he had to do was sit through this lecture and then fill in a few forms. Once you were on the scheme, no one gave a toss about whether or not you made a serious attempt to earn a living from self-employment. Most of the concerns set up under the auspices of the EAS failed when the weekly subsidy was withdrawn at the end of the first year's trading. The government didn't give a fuck. As long as it appeared that the dole queues were being cut, then Honourable Members held their peace. For all the hot air these wankers expended on the subject, Terry had yet to be convinced there was a single Westminster careerist who was genuinely concerned about the plight of the working man.

Miss Dobbs had completed her opening address. Now, one at a time, everyone in the room was introducing themselves and outlining the type of business they hoped to set up.

'Scum-sucker,' Terry muttered under his breath as yet another long-haired tosser pontificated over the prospects of pursuing a career as an artist.

'Sorry I'm late,' a scruffy bird in denims mouthed as she came through the door. The chick pulled out the chair next to Terry and flopped into it.

'Well, young lady,' Dobbs spat the words through pursed lips, 'I'm not sure whether I can let you attend this seminar. You're nearly half an hour late.'

'I misread the address,' the girl explained. 'I went to Commercial Road instead of coming to Commercial Street.'

'You're fortunate that I'm a charitable Christian woman who's prepared to give street-urchins a second chance.'

'Thanks,' the girl hissed sarcastically.

'Now, where was I?' Dobbs continued. 'Oh yes, we're here to discuss each of you setting up a small business with generous help from the government.'

'I don't call forty quid a week generous,' the late arrival mumbled.

Terry turned and flashed the girl a smile. She winked back. The bird had obviously got herself mixed up in the punk-hippy cross-over. Her long hair was bleached blonde but showed very light brown for three inches at the roots. She needed a bath and a clean set of clothes. Despite the filth, Terry was more than willing to seduce the chick. Perhaps with his help she'd see the error of her ways and convert to a skin-girl crop and regular bathing habits. Although hippies had always provided boot-boys with heads to bash, Blake often found himself attracted to the female of the breed. He knew from experience they were both willing and easy. And this particular bird was skinny and flat-chested just the way Terry liked 'em.

'Terribly sorry I'm late, had a spot of bother getting out of bed,' a well-dressed young man announced as he strode into the room.

'Just sit yourself down there,' Dobbs said, pointing to a chair.

'Fuckin' typical,' the hippy swore. 'She gives 'im an easy time just 'coz 'ee's middle class.'

Terry put his hand on the girl's thigh.

'My name's Joyce,' the hippy whispered.

'Terry,' Blake replied.

'Perhaps the best way to pay your National Insurance is by banker's order,' Dobbs suggested. 'You can instruct your bank to pay it every two weeks. It's important not to get behind with these contributions because otherwise you might be faced with a bill you can ill afford to pay at the end of the year.'

'Bollocks!' Terry interjected. 'You're tellin' us that 'coz you're a representative of the ruling class. You've been instructed to give us bad advice. The government just wants to take back with one hand what it gives us with the other! Anyone with any brains will defer paying tax and NI for as long as possible. Regular suppliers of goods and services are the only people a businessman needs to keep sweet with prompt settlements. On one-off deals and government rake-offs the smart trader holds out on even the smallest payment. The money can be used to improve his cash-flow or stashed in an investment account where it'll make interest. Personally, I'm gonna apply for exemption from NI on the grounds of low income. That way, even if I make a packet from my first year of trading, I can hold out on paying contributions for a long, long, time.'

'You have a bad attitude.' Dobbs retorted in an icy voice.

'So what?' Terry hissed. 'Why can't we be honest about this? The bullshit you've been spouting about business being good for the community makes me sick. Let's face it, capitalism's a rat race. I was 'appy enough on the dole, but since I'm being sucked into your cesspool of money-making I'm gonna 'ave to be ruthless to come out on top. The Tories calling for an enterprise culture is a fuckin' joke. Anyone who sets up in business without realizing they live in a rip-off culture is gonna go under – and fast!'

Blake quickly lost interest in what Dobbs had to say by way of reply because Joyce was touching him up. He felt his prick hardening as the hippy played with his balls. He wanted to rip down his trousers and luxuriate in skin-to-skin contact. Joyce moved her hand upwards and clasped Terry's shaft. Having felt Blake's excitement, the hippy let her fingers slide down his crotch and resumed her game of billiards.

Another woman had been introduced to the class and was midway through some bullshit speech about the joys of self-employment. Terry didn't have a clue what she'd been talking about but felt certain of his ability to denounce her line in pro-enterprise rhetoric, had he listened to the lies tumbling from her mouth. Joyce's hand was resting on his love muscle. The girl was a fuckin' tease! The skinhead was visualizing what he'd do with the hippy at the end of their EAS induction. Joyce would tug down his flies and give out a little gasp when she noticed he was wearing Union Jack briefs. Then she'd pull Terry's prick out of his pants and swallow the swollen member. As her mouth moved up and down Blake's shaft, she'd smear his love muscle with lipstick. With her right hand working the base of his manhood, Joyce made Terry come inside her mouth. She swallowed most of the semen, allowing what was left to dribble down her chin. Terry imagined kissing Joyce and being able to taste his own come on her lips.

Terry decided to try a change of fantasy. This time he imagined that, as Joyce sucked him off, he was reading aloud from the *Economic and Philosophic Manuscripts of 1844* by Marx. He visualized her tongue moving over the tip of his cock and activating a DNA code buried deep inside his cortex. Fighting against the genetic forces which would mobilize to seize control of his bulk, he'd recite the opening lines of this seminal work: *The antagonistic struggle between capitalist and worker determines wages. . . .* Joyce was trying to force her tongue inside Blake's cock, pushing it into the tiny piss-hole at the tip. Terry wanted to scream out in ecstasy but checked the impulse. He was engaged in a demonstration of Determination and Will. He would continue with his recitation: *Necessarily victory goes to the capitalist. The capitalist can survive longer without the worker than the worker can live without the capitalist. Combination among the capitalists is natural and effective; whereas combination among workers is prohibited and has unpleasant consequences for them.*

Terry was getting really steamed up. He thought Marx was terrific, but there were also many other authors he wanted to recite as Joyce sucked him off. The skinhead imagined he was spilling his seed into the hippy's mouth as he recited the *SCUM Manifesto.* He wondered if it would be better to declaim a little Andrea Dworkin. Blake got off on the idea of introducing working-class birds to feminist theory as they gave him head. Trendies occasionally accused the boot-boy of being sexist. Despite close study of the *Anti-Oedipus*, these wankers had yet to understand that come culture was the ultimate in fluid discourse.

After the lesson in women's liberation the skin and the hippy would indulge in really deep sex. It would start slowly with both of them lying on their sides. Terry'd hump for ten minutes before reaching out for a tube of KY. He'd squeeze the jell over his fingers and proceed to rub it into Joyce's arse. Terry's cock would be moving in and out of the hippy's cunt, it wouldn't seem unnatural when a finger penetrated her sphincter. Soon there'd be two, and then three fingers traversing her rim of dark pleasures. Terry'd pull his hand free of the hippy's arse and spin her around, so that she'd end up face down on the bed.

'That's my cunt,' Joyce murmured as he slipped back inside her.

'I know,' Terry replied.

'I thought you wanted my arse,' Joyce whispered.

'I do,' her top replied, 'but that comes a little bit later.'

Terry sniffed his fingers. He liked the smell of the girl's arse. He pulled himself free of her cunt and rammed his cock against her sphincter. The love muscle slithered along Joyce's rim. Blake wrapped his left arm around the hippy's waist. With his right hand he guided his cock into her arse. He rammed the love muscle home. Joyce spat phlegm as he penetrated her anal rim.

'Are you OK?' Terry asked, unsure of himself.

'Yeah,' Joyce replied.

'I don't wanna hurt you,' Blake whispered.

'I don't care what you do, I just wanna feel you come inside me,' Joyce insisted.

Terry began to pump up the volume. He stuck his fingers into Joyce's mouth so she could groove on the taste of her own shit. The rhythm with which they made love became increasingly strident. Blake could feel love juice boiling through his prick.

Terry was woken from this wet dream by the sound of chair legs scraping across the floor. Joyce had removed her hand from his lap and like everyone else she'd turned around to look at a TV screen. The video they were watching was about the joys of running your own business. Susan had set herself up as a self-employed hairdresser. She didn't have her own premises and so she attended to her clients' coiffure in their homes. The next video was about some idiot who dreamt of making a fortune as a quality chocolate manufacturer. His business staggered from disaster to disaster and Terry had high hopes that the bastard would top himself as he faced financial ruin. Unfortunately, the scum-sucker pulled through these difficulties and turned his venture into a money-spinning success.

After they'd watched this completely uninspiring propaganda for enterprise culture, it was time for the class to get a free lunch. This turned out to be egg sandwiches with a choice of tea or coffee. Terry gobbled down some food and then followed Joyce out of the room as she announced she was going to the toilet.

The hippy was aroused by the idea of taking a man into the ladies. To Blake it was old hat, he'd done this a million times before. He looked at the girl sitting on the toilet, her 501s around her ankles, then sniffed the air which was pungent with the odour of bleach.

'Get your tits out,' Terry ordered.

Joyce took off her denim jacket and handed it to Blake. He hung it on a peg screwed to the cubicle door. The hippy pulled off her T-shirt and wiped it under her arms and between her legs before swabbing Terry's face with the filthy rag. When she'd finished, Blake hung the T-shirt over the girl's denim jacket. All the while he'd been assessing the hippy's knockers. She was virtually flat-chested, which pleased the boot-boy no end. He'd always had a weakness for girls who looked like boys.

'I wanna watch you piss.' Terry spoke the words in an even tone.

'I've got an idea,' Joyce announced as she took off her sneakers. 'I'm gonna pee in your mouth.'

'You what?' Terry asked, startled.

'I'm gonna piss on your face,' Joyce said as she removed her Levis.

'But I'm the top!' Terry insisted.

'We're role-playing and the roles can be reversed,' Joyce retorted. 'I don't go in for this middle-class line against objectification. Good sex requires objectification. Sexism only exists when one gender escapes the process. I'm not about to let that happen because I'm turning you into my toilet.'

As she said this, Joyce clambered on to the cistern. She balanced herself by resting her hands on the dividers that separated her cubicle from those adjacent to it. Then the hippy stuck her bum out so she could piss into the bog.

'Put your head over the bowl and look up at my arse,' she ordered.

Desiring his oats, Terry felt he had no option but to obey.

'Open your mouth,' Joyce commanded in an authoritarian tone.

The first burst of piss hit Terry in the eye.

'Sussed birds exercise their bladder by calling a halt half-way through whenever they take a leak,' Joyce explained. 'It strengthens the muscles and means you retain control of 'em as you get older. I've stuck to this routine for years 'coz I sure as hell don't wanna end up an incontinent old hag.'

Joyce opened her bladder and this time she was on target. A torrent of piss sloshed into Terry's mouth. Blake gulped down a portion of the golden fluid while allowing the excess to gush over his lips, run down the side of his face and splash into the toilet.

'Stand up,' Joyce ordered, once she'd finished.

Terry obeyed. Leaning back against the cubicle door he savoured the warm sensation in the back of his throat, the sweet after-taste of the hippy's steaming discharge.

Joyce climbed down from the cistern and pulled on her 501s.

'But I wanna fuck you,' Terry complained.

'Later,' Joyce snapped. 'First I'm gonna take a good look at your dick. You're gonna be inspected for disease!'

She put her hand on Blake's flies and undid them. When Joyce saw his Union Jack briefs she let out a short gasp of horror. Roberts had told her to investigate Blake's links to a libertarian terror group. Terry's name had been found in an address book belonging to a member of Makhno's Anarchist Army. The undercover agent decided she might as well close the case. Rather than being a comrade of Red bombers, her subject was apparently a supporter of the far-Right.

'I don't fuck fascists,' Joyce said coldly.

'Who said I was a fascist?' Terry demanded.

'You're wearing Union Jack underpants!' was her reply.

'So what?' Terry snapped as he banged a fist into his palm. 'I want you to know I'm a committed communist cadre! I'm not ashamed of the fact that I come from a non-proletarian background. My mum and dad were both secondary-school teachers and so my social origins are lower middle class. Caught in the vice of class conflict, born neither as a worker nor to rule, I embraced the revolutionary cause and accepted in full the consequences of this choice. Without any regard for my personal welfare, I became a communist intellectual. As Sorel taught us, regardless of social origin, revolutionary theorists must necessarily be considered petty bourgeois. As such, rather than seeing myself as constituting some mythical vanguard, I've accepted a secondary role in the fight for socialism and devoted my energies to discrediting the ruling culture. As a communist intellectual it's my task to challenge the prestige of those values which inhibit the growth of class consciousness. In pursuit of this noble ideal I've spent long hours studying how the workers resist embourgeoisement. Consequently I'm conversant with the tactics proletarians adopt to prevent their culture being assimilated by the upper classes. I've paid particular attention to skinhead subculture and my research eventually led me to the conclusion that anyone who seriously adopts a hard-line materialist critique must eventually become a boot-boy.'

'But why do you wear Union Jack briefs?' Joyce demanded.

'Because', Terry replied, 'I came to realize that the majority of boot-boys aren't nationalists at all! You only have to listen to Oi records to see that most skinhead bands possess a fully developed class consciousness. Take a group like The Last Resort, whose songs are nothing less than anthems to the concept of class struggle. The band in question also used a fair amount of antiquated nationalist imagery and even recorded a song entitled 'Red, White and Blue'. On the level of appearances this implies theoretical ineptitude. Fascists imagine the nation constitutes a single mythic community. Oi music rubs against the grain of far-Right thinking because class divisions form an explicit part of skinhead culture. Unless we assume that skins are thick, boot-boys are consciously using a discredited form of imperialism to scare off liberals and protect their culture from assimilation by the ruling class.'

'I still don't understand why you're sporting nationalist under-wear,' the hippy snorted.

'Because', Blake persisted, 'by adopting the symbols of the English ruling class, skins are bringing all the badges of power into disrepute. A symbol derives its commonly understood meaning from a specific set of associations. In the case of the Union Jack, these associations are displays of power on the part of the English ruling class. By persistently placing the British flag outside such a context, skins are attacking the very basis of this standard's power. If my guess is right, pretty soon the Union Jack will be completely discredited as a symbol. Boot-boys have learnt a great deal from the wholesale adoption of communist chic by middle-class trendies. The ruling culture has deprived the workers of numerous symbols by turning them into meaningless fashion accessories. By wearing Union Jacks, skinheads are turning this tactic against those who first used it as a weapon in the class war. Since it's the task of the proletariat to organize and carry out the class struggle, revolutionary intellectuals can only follow their lead. That's why I'm wearing a pair of Union Jack briefs!'

'What if skinheads 'ave got it all wrong?' Joyce wanted to know.

'The workers are always right!' Terry insisted.

'But supposing Roi Pearce of The Last Resort and the boot-boys who buy his records are just plain thick?' Joyce persisted. 'What if these skinheads are sincere patriots who don't realize their equally genuine pride in being working class is incompatible with their nationalist beliefs?'

'It doesn't matter,' Terry reassured her. 'Eventually the developing contradictions of class society will bring them round to my way of thinking.'

'Isn't that a rigidly deterministic position?' the hippy countered. 'After all, shouldn't there be a place for free choice and voluntary action within the revolutionary programme? Hasn't the communist Left always emphasized the centrality of the autonomous subject to its vision of a post-capitalist society?'

'You're right!' Terry admitted. 'And as punishment for being such a smart arse, you can get on your knees and suck my cock.'

Joyce felt she had no choice but to obey. After all, if she wanted to pass herself off as a communist militant, she'd have to demonstrate that at heart she too was an anti-intellectual. The hippy put her hand into Blake's briefs and took out his love muscle.

Terry loved the way it felt when a chick primed his genetic pump. When he was eleven, Blake had let a queue of girls put their hands down his trousers. Since no other boy in his school would admit to letting birds size them up, Terry landed himself a reputation as a pervert. From that day to this, Blake considered it a bizarre quirk of patriarchal society that blokes boasted of fingering the female sex but tended to keep quiet about their genetic exploits when these consisted of no more than a hand job.

'How does it taste?' Terry asked Joyce as she put his prick into her mouth.

'Of cock,' she replied before closing her lips around his sweaty manhood.

Joyce kept her hand clasped around the base of Blake's love muscle. She wasn't prepared to take it all the way down her throat. Terry was happy enough with the way she worked the shaft. All he asked for in life was the chance to recite passages of communist propaganda while million-year-old genetic codes fought to control his bulk: *People who talk about revolution and class struggle. . . .* Terry stumbled with the quote from *The*

Revolution of Everyday Life by Raoul Vaneigem. He would never escape the Dictatorship of the DNA but nevertheless enjoyed struggling against it until his brain was so saturated with endorphins that it became impossible to carry on the fight: *. . . without, without referring . . . explicitly. . . .*

Blake's brain clouded over and then clarity returned for a full minute: *. . . to everyday life, without understanding what is subversive about love and what is positive in the refusal of constraints, such people have a corpse in their mouth. . . .*

Then Terry lost all conscious control of his body and mind. He was no longer aware that Joyce was pumping up the volume as she beat out the collectivist rhythm of sex. All the fetters of capitalist restriction had fallen away. Blake had passed beyond the subject/object duality and for a brief moment experienced communism as an orgasmic truth. Human relations had not only become completely transparent, they'd actually ceased to exist, since Terry's self was dissolved in collectivized consciousness. Communism and the sexual ecstasy that accompanied it went beyond petty individualism. It was the movement of vast majorities unfettered by the apparatus of a state!

Joyce took Blake's cock out of her mouth and increased the tempo with which she was beating the meat. Terry experienced orgasm as an action replay of the revolutionary uprising in Russia, 1905. Love juice boiled through his prick like workers pouring out of a factory after a mass meeting has decided on a strike.

Joyce ducked and liquid DNA shot over her head. Blake groaned and slumped against the cubicle door. For a moment he was convinced he was leading a proletarian uprising. As a phalanx of workers followed him into the breach, the over-powering smell of bleach distracted his attention. Terry opened his eyes and saw his spunk dribbling on to the floor.

'You didn't let me come in your mouth, bitch!' he swore.

'So what?' Joyce replied.

'It means I can't taste myself when I kiss you,' Terry spat as he bent forward and pressed his mouth against the girl's lips.

'You eat too much curry and spice,' the hippy said as she broke the kiss. 'If you hadn't ruined your taste-buds, you'd still catch the sweaty flavour of your cock in my mouth.'

'Bollocks!' Blake snorted.

'Come on,' Joyce hissed as she grabbed a wad of tissue and wiped Terry down. 'I wanna get another cuppa before the afternoon session begins.'

'But I wanna fuck you!' Terry protested.

'Later,' Joyce said as she pulled on her filthy T-shirt.

'Now!' Terry insisted.

'Listen,' Joyce snarled, 'chewin' your cock is thirsty work, and if we don't go back now there won't be time for another cuppa.'

'Will you go home with me after class?' Blake demanded.

'Sure,' the hippy replied as she hung her denim jacket over an arm.

Terry pulled up his trousers. Joyce opened the door and hauled Blake out of the cubicle. The boot-boy insisted that they flush the loo and wash their hands before leaving the ladies.

Back in the classroom the supply of tea had run out and so Joyce had to drink coffee. Three egg sandwiches remained uneaten. Thinking waste was criminal, Blake scoffed the lot.

'Where did you two go?' asked the girl who'd been sitting next to Joyce during the morning session.

'To the ladies.' Terry replied.

'What did you do there?' the bird wanted to know.

'I sucked him off,' the hippy informed her.

'Can I give him head later?' the girl demanded.

'Proposition him, darling, don't ask me about it!' Joyce said, never imagining that this middle-class bitch would have the nerve to do so.

'Excuse me, Terry.' The girl spoke in the softest of tones. 'My name's Marion Calder. I noticed you were eyeing me up before your friend came in this morning. Do you think it would be possible for the two of us to indulge in a touch of the old physical later?'

'Here's my card,' Terry replied as he pulled the slip from his pocket and handed it to Marion. 'Call me up and make an appointment.'

'Terry Blake,' she said reading aloud, 'Film and Video, 210 Kelson House, Manchester Road, Isle of Dogs, London E14, telephone 071 533 9991.'

'That's me!' the boot-boy assured her.

'And you make film and video,' Marion said, awestruck.

'That's right,' Terry replied.

'Can I be in one of your films?' Marion demanded.

'Sure,' Terry replied. 'I'm making an interesting series with a role that's made for you. It's all done hand held on super 8. I've had various birds and blokes suck me off while I filmed their antics. Of course the pictures are pretty shaky, but the results are interesting and . . .'

'Oh, wow!' Marion interjected. 'I'm gonna be in the movies! You can come in my mouth any time. . . .'

Terry wondered whether Marion's declaration of sexual submission would annoy Joyce. If it did, then that was just too bad. He'd never been the type to resist birds who made open passes at him.

Terry didn't pay any attention to the woman, who spent the afternoon explaining how she'd set up her own business wholesaling cashew nuts to health food stores. Common sense told him that this bird had never earned more than a bread-and-butter living from such ventures, since anyone who had a genuine instinct for money-making wouldn't squander their talents picking up spare change on a government-backed small business scheme. Besides, Blake had other things on his mind, such as the fun and games he'd organize for Marion once she'd booked herself a sex session in his Docklands pad. She seemed like the kind of woman who dreamt of having a top piss up her arse. Terry felt it was high time he tested this trick on a bird. All twelve blokes who'd received similar treatment found it a real turn-on when combined with a number of other suitably exotic sexual practices.

Fortunately, no one asked any questions at the end of the enterprise induction. Each member of the class was given an application form for the EAS, and then everyone was dismissed.

'Give me a buzz,' Blake said to Marion after kissing her on the lips.

The boot-boy wanted to rid himself of the girl. His immediate concern was to get Joyce over to his flat. He was hell-bent on filming the action as he got his dick back into the hippy's mouth. Terry had spent much of the afternoon considering how to frame the perfect come shot. He'd more or less cracked the problem and wanted to set to work on what he felt had the potential to be a masterpiece of bad taste.

'Let's go,' Blake said to Joyce.

'Go where?' the hippy demanded.

'Home,' he replied.

'I've gotta get some blow first,' Joyce spat defiantly. 'My dealer's been on holiday for a week and I'm gasping for a smoke.'

Blake groaned. He should have guessed this bird would have a degenerate drug habit. Personally, Terry felt nothing but contempt for those who smoked hash. He only took stimulants that made him harder and more violent. Speed was the true proletarian drug. The inroads dope had made on the recreational habits of working-class youth was deeply depressing. Too many estate kids were sitting around crash pads getting mellow over a smoke when they should have been out rucking the filth or smashing up some rich bastard's car.

Two

Hackney's front line runs from Kingsland High Street to Amhurst Road, hitting the latter near the Dalston Lane junction. It lies uneasily between the north and east axes of the city. This is Sandringham Road, where black entrepeneurs dressed in smart sportswear sell pot to the hippy scum who flood into London's Giro Borough.

Years ago, when Terry lived in Stoke Newington, he'd signed on at the dole office in Spurstowe Terrace. On the walk down to his fortnightly meeting with a representative of what was then known as the DHSS, he'd often been accosted by a black kid trying to sell hash. The fact that anyone could mistake him for one of the unwashed horde who might buy a bag was deeply mortifying to Blake. Had he not possessed a materialist critique of the reigning society, this was an experience which could have turned him into a racist. Fortunately, Terry understood that black youth were playing a vital role in the class struggle. They sold a particularly degenerate element within the middle class the means of its self-destruction.

'I've gotta call someone up,' Blake told his pick-up. 'You can score on your own. I'll meet you by the phone-box outside Hackney Downs station.'

'OK,' Joyce assented.

As he turned the corner into Wayland Avenue, Terry felt a deep sense of relief. He'd not let the hippy compromise him. There was no way he'd go and score dope with a pick-up. Drugs, as they say, is for hippies.

When Blake reached the call-box and saw what was going on inside, he rubbed his eyes to make sure he wasn't seeing things. A man in his mid-fifties was inserting a piece of torn card into the phone's change slot. Terry was amazed that anyone still practised this old trick. The con had been so well publicized that for years the first thing Blake did when a box swallowed his dosh was to check the coin return slot to make sure it hadn't been jammed by some joker who was hell bent on picking up the change. The grifter shuffled nervously and lifted the receiver, hoping that this action would convince Blake he'd been making a call.

Terry hauled the bastard out into the street and kicked him on the shin.

'Don't hurt me,' the old codger pleaded as he hopped up and down on one foot.

'You deserve to die,' Terry spat, 'ripping off your own people, your own class. The yuppies who've moved in round 'ere have phones in their homes. It's only the poor who use call-boxes in places like this.'

'Don't get excited, son!' the grifter protested. 'I only rip-off change in areas where there's a lot of immigrants. I'm only taking back what ethnics have stolen from us in muggings and burglaries. . . .'

Blake slammed his fist into the racist's mouth. There was the satisfying crunch of splintering bone and the bastard staggered backwards, spitting gouts of blood and the occasional piece of broken tooth. Four youths rushed up to join in the fun. They pushed Terry out of the way and let loose with their steel toe-capped DMs. The felled racist could feel the boots raining in against his ageing flesh. Blow after blow sent waves of agony surging through his bulk. Muffled moans lost themselves down Dalston Lane as the youths chanted 'Bogside, Clydeside, Join the Angry Side!'

The grifter was overcome by an all-pervasive numbness which rendered him insensitive to the terrible toll being wreaked upon his body. He sank deeper and deeper into the blackness, thankful for the opportunity it afforded him to escape the pain of this beating.

'Throw 'im in the phone-box,' Terry ordered. 'That way it'll take longer till 'e's found.'

'Smart thinking!' replied one of the youths.

'We've been after that bastard Brian Smith for a long time,' said another.

Suddenly Terry realized why these boys were treating him like a hero. Without even realizing it, he'd done over one of Britain's most notorious fascist organizers, the Führer of a tiny Third Positionist sect known as Cockney Nation. These lunatics professed a creed that called for the transformation of the London boroughs of Hackney, Tower Hamlets and Newham into an all-white state. Cockney Nation would be the first of many patriotic corporations which the most marginalized elements on the far-Right saw as constituting an England of One Hundred Flags. Add in Scotland, Ulster, Wales, Kernow, Mannin and Eire and you had the complete British Family of Nations!

'Let's introduce ourselves,' said one of the youths. 'I'm Rodney James.'

'I'm Arnold Chance,' said another.

'I'm Raymond Nicolson,' said the third.

'I'm Sebastian Nicolson,' said the last.

'Along with Rupert Dawson-Rand, we make up the membership of the theoretically coherent group My One Flesh. We're fighting for a situationist revolution,' Rodney concluded rather pompously.

'I'm Terry Blake,' Terry told them, 'and I say the revolution is fuckin' yer woman until she can't stand up!'

'Hear, hear,' My One Flesh responded in unison. Then they looked at each other rather sheepishly, hoping this unfortunate turn of phrase hadn't betrayed their upper-class origins. Having run into what they took to be a theoretically coherent prole, the last thing they wanted to do was alienate this prize catch. Several backward anarchist groups boasted a postal worker, and one even a dustman, within their ranks. My One Flesh were determined to recruit a member who'd come up from the slime and the factory grime. The support of a manual labourer would do wonders for their credibility.

'Ooohhh,' Joyce said as she came up behind Terry and grabbed his arm, 'you've got me a line-up!'

'You up to the crack?' Terry asked the comrades.

'What crack?' Rodney inquired innocently. 'And why don't you introduce us to your girl-friend?'

'I'm Joyce Grant,' the hippy chimed, 'and what me and Terry were asking was if you were into a gang-bang.'

'You . . . you . . . you mean you want us all to make love to you?' Rodney stammered.

'I want you to fuck me until I can't stand up!' Joyce spat provocatively.

'That's . . . that's a tall order,' Rodney croaked. 'None of us have ever done it with a girl.'

'Yes, we have,' Raymond lied. 'We gang-bang a tart every Saturday night. It's just you've always been too far gone after our heavy sessions in The Tanners to participate in the sexual athletics.'

'We'll service you, miss,' Sebastian reassured Joyce.

'You should meet our leader . . .' Arnold put in.

'Shut up,' Raymond snapped. 'Situationists don't have leaders, we're autonomous subjects.'

'You're right,' Arnold admitted. 'But Joyce should meet Comrade Rupert. He's such a randy sod, he's been in more special clinics than you've had hot dinners.'

'Let's not hang about, then,' Joyce implored. 'You've all agreed we're gonna gang-bang. Let's climb on to the railway embankment and bonk.'

'But people going by in the trains will be able to see us,' Rodney protested.

'Shut up,' Blake spat.

'We squat in Graham Road,' Sebastian put in, 'we could all go there.'

'Oh, alright,' Terry and Joyce agreed reluctantly.

Raymond led the troops off the Dalston Lane battlefield. His three comrades lagged behind their new-found friends and from this rearguard position eyed up the hippy's arse. As they shuffled off, muffled moans could be heard coming from the callbox. Brian Smith was evidently regaining consciousness.

'This ain't a fuckin' squat!' Blake shouted as Raymond ushered him into a renovated terrace. 'Whose dad bought it for them?'

'OK, so it isn't a squat,' Ray admitted. 'Sebastian and I purchased it with money we inherited from our grandparents.'

Satisfied he'd proved the superiority of his own will to that of these upper-class dolts, Terry stripped off. He noticed the admiring glances his slim but well-toned body caught from the four pro-situs. Blake guessed correctly that these ex-public-school boys had done plenty of corn-balling but were bereft of heterosexual experience.

Joyce rolled a joint, then pulled off her T-shirt and revealed her tits. Having taken several drags on the reefer, the hippy offered Terry a toke. He shook his head, so she passed the joint to Raymond.

Arnold was pouring treble Hundred Pipers. Dutch courage for the comrades. Rodney stared at Joyce in disbelief. It came as a shock to his system to be confronted by a nude woman.

22

Sebastian slipped a CD of Beethoven's Ninth into an overpriced hi-fi system.

''Aven't you got anything but classical crap?' Terry complained.

'I'm sorry,' Sebastian simpered, 'but we don't own any pop records.'

'I usually fuck to "Death in June" or "Laibach",' Blake informed him. 'Can't you pull out a Monty Python record or something?'

'I'm ashamed to admit', the pro-situ mumbled, 'that we only have classical items in our collection.'

Joyce kicked off her shoes, Terry dropped his trousers. Saliva dripped from Rodney's mouth as the polymorphous perverts proceeded with their strip de luxe. Having disrobed, Joyce got on her knees and licked the tip of Terry's cock.

'I want you,' she said. 'I want you inside me. I want you to dominate me. I wanna feel your cock, feel you using me. I wanna seek out my genetic destiny!'

'No problem,' Blake said as he pulled Joyce to the floor.

To Rodney this was a truly incredible scene. He couldn't believe that members of the lower classes were so uninhibited that they'd screw in front of him without being paid for providing this entertainment. Arnold swallowed his treble and then took a swig straight from the Hundred Pipers bottle. Raymond snatched the whisky from him and gulped down a mouthful.

The atmosphere in the room was electric. The four pro-situs were overcome by terror as they prepared for their initiation into the mysteries of female desire. The bottle of Hundred Pipers was passed from shaking hand to shaking hand as My One Flesh desperately attempted to straighten themselves out before participating in their first bisexual marathon. Joyce was well juiced up and Terry slipped into her with the ease of a Channel ferry docking at Dover.

In and out Blake pounded to the sound of Beethoven's Ninth. While the classical music told the story of bourgeois ascendancy, the slapping of flesh against flesh spoke of older and greater legends. Out of the darkness came an explosion of light, and life was sent crashing through the universe. The evolutionary developments from swamp culture to human culture were recounted in the blink of an eye. Then there was the first heroic phase of primitive communism followed by slave societies and feudalism. Terry and Joyce had reached the period of reaction praised by Ludwig Van in his hymn to the ultra-violence of the German Conservative Tradition. This was a plea for the freedom of the individual to be realized in the ideal of the Nation State. In a vain attempt to escape class divisions and the world-shaking implications of the French Revolution, the seeds of Nazism found expression in a desire to impose a dictatorship of poets and philosophers.

Terry and Joyce pumped up the volume, their limbs flailing as they writhed in ecstasy on the carpet. The orgasm which shot through their twin bulks was a clarion call for workers' revolution and an insight into the new era of communism which would follow this Invisible Insurrection of Ten Billion Minds. It would be the movement of vast majorities unfettered by the apparatus of a state; a system based on organic centralism rather than the discredited democratic variant. Joyce could feel Terry's love juice oozing out of her cunt. She thrilled at the thought of the four pro-situs riding into her on this sea of liquid genetics. Together they would blaze a trail to a new way of life!

Blake rose from the floor. Joyce mentally prepared herself to receive the next supplicant. The ex-public-school boys were still fully dressed. Rodney was salivating like a rabid dog. Terry grabbed him by the collar and flung him to the ground. The pro-situ's head ended up between the hippy's well-spread legs.

'Eat and be damned,' Terry ordered.

Rodney obeyed, concentrating on the unique flavour of Blake's liquid genetics and doing his best to ignore the strange taste of the girl's sex.

'Lick me, lick me clean,' Joyce was moaning. 'Come on, you brainless prick, get your tongue into my cunt!'

Terry walked over to Raymond. He looked the youth up and down and was less than impressed by the way this substandard product of inbreeding and poisoned genes attempted to keep his cool. 'You don't have to say please,' Terry informed him. 'Get down on your knees and suck my cock.'

Raymond didn't need a second invitation. He'd been trained to respect charismatic leadership and responded instantly with submission. He took Blake's love muscle in his mouth and wondered whether this unique tool – which had been ritually denounced on hundreds of occasions by anti-porn protesters – was not, in fact, the old mole with which Marx had threatened the bourgeoisie.

Terry smiled as he took in the envious gaze Sebastian had fixed upon his brother. 'My face could launch a thousand ships,' he anounced, 'and burn the topless towers of Ilium. My cock draws forth men's souls. See, see where they fly. . . .'

Arnold fled from the room and locked himself in the downstairs toilet. As he parked his arse on the plastic seat, he reflected that he'd always been an individualist at heart. Arnold wasn't prepared to let the others define his sexuality for him. He'd never joined in when the comrades corn-balled and was certain that the joys of the gang-bang were not for him. He was an auto-sexual, someone who wanted a free hand in constructing his own – absolutely unique – erotic identity. In the past, when the comrades dismissed his position on the sexual question as a load of old wank, Arnold contented himself with the thought that it was he – and not the sceptics – who'd placed his hands on the deeper mysteries of life. After witnessing the scene in the living-room, he felt his instinctive beliefs in relation to this issue had been thoroughly vindicated. Arnold was satisfied that his own bulk was infinitely more beautiful than the bodies of the unwashed masses.

'Get stuck into my arse!' Terry ordered Sebastian.

It was as if the submissive pro-situ had been given an insight into untrammelled desire by Debord himself. There was the happiest of airs about him as he administered the rim job. The taste of Terry's shit did something for this misfit's soul. To someone from a background as privileged as Sebastian's, Blake was as proletarian as pie 'n' mash. To be licking at lower-class dirt eased the pro-situ's feelings of guilt about his family's vast financial holdings. On top of this, he was excited by the prospect of Terry giving it to him up the arse. It had been a lifelong ambition on Sebastian's part to be fucked senseless by a horny-handed son of toil.

'You don't have to suck my cunt dry!' Joyce squealed at Rodney as she slipped her hands under his armpits and pulled him upwards.

Their mouths met and the hippy could taste herself on Rodney's lips. He seemed to be having trouble getting his cock into her cunt, so Joyce put her hand around the swollen love muscle and guided this sweet meat into the inner mystery of her being. Here the pro-situ discovered an emptiness which he was determined to fill with ecstatic memories of their origin.

Unfortunately, Rodney didn't have a clue about how he should proceed with his genetic mission and the hippy had to thrust herself against him until he took the hint and began to beat out the primitive rhythm which held them in the thrall of the Almighty DNA.

Rodney had left Hackney, had left this world, to become a qualitatively different being. He'd abandoned the physical for the metaphysical, lower values for higher values. In Rodney's feeble imagination, the becoming of the proletariat entailed his metamorphosis into a philosopher-warrior who'd fight for communism. Perhaps one day he'd abandon ideology altogether and replace it with a hard-line materialist critique. Then he'd see that his place within the class struggle was with the mass, that so-called intellectuals did not occupy a privileged position in relation to the working class. Once he'd learnt this from hard knocks in the school of life, he'd also realize that there were no longer any values worth defending. The mass would arise and sweep aside the hierarchy of value.

After weakening his mind with poisonous situationist texts, young Rodney had succumbed to Debord's ridiculous system of half-truths and lies. Had he been a son of the working class, he'd have known instinctively that lucidity is a state of beliefflessness.

Joyce had no time for Rodney's abstractions. As a street-hardened proletarian and state-employed spy who rarely moved outside the most lumpen of circles, she knew that the task of the communist intellectual was to ruin the existing culture. If Rodney had been a genuine militant, he'd have been discrediting all received ideas without putting anything in their place. Instead, he was turning her off with his ridiculous pillow talk about the central role intellectuals played in the development of the revolutionary struggle. His antics brought to mind a poster she'd once seen proclaiming *Sisters, make love to revolutionaries!* Rodney was no different to the bozos who'd issued this call, an imbecile more in need of sexual therapy than a proletarian revolution with unlicensed pleasure as its only aim.

Blake was on top of Sebastian. He was grinding his mount into the ground as he beat out the collectivist rhythm of sex. Raymond knelt above Sebastian's head, thrusting his cock ever deeper into his brother's throat, until he finally fired a wad of molten genetics into this welcoming hole. To Sebastian, this standard issue DNA tasted like the sweetest of nectars. It was a pre-revolutionary manifestation of the ever-growing ecstasy that would lead to the realization of wo/man's orgasmic potential. Sex was a clarion call for a communist disorder to be imposed on this world of illusion.

Sebastian didn't know whether the cock in his arse belonged to Terry or himself. Regardless of ownership, it was discharging an enormous wad of liquid DNA. Now that this offering to their genetic destiny had been lodged at the very centre of his being, Sebastian wanted to feel something even bigger penetrate his rim of dark pleasures. As soon as Raymond removed the cock from his mouth, he would beg to be fisted!

Joyce could feel Rodney coming inside her. However, the pro-situ didn't cut it as a sexual athlete and his exertions were worth less than nothing to a woman as experienced as the hippy nymphomaniac.

'Next!' Joyce shouted as Rodney rose from her bulk.

Raymond removed his cock from his brother's mouth and shuffled over to the girl. He grabbed the hippy by the shoulders and spun her round so that she was lying with her face buried in the carpet.

'I want you to fuck my cunt,' Joyce said in a rather muffled voice.

'No problem,' Raymond replied. 'I'd prefer your arse which, I must say, looks very tight. However, if you want me to probe your rice pudding like sex, I'll oblige. But stay lying on your stomach, so I don't have to look at your girlish face.'

'Listen, bimbo,' Joyce retorted, 'you could just as easily close your eyes and obtain the same result. Let's face it, you prefer this position because it's more dominant. Now let's just get on with it.'

The pro-situ admitted he'd been out-argued by remaining silent and shoving his cock into the moist mystery of Joyce's sex. This gateway to motherhood offered little resistance to his throbbing love muscle. In Raymond's opinion, there was no pleasure to be taken from the resultant pushing and shoving. He got off on beating his partner into submission, on forcing a passage between tight walls of flesh. The exchange of bodily fluids meant less than nothing to Raymond. What mattered was the fight and a top's ability to dominate any masochist who writhed beneath his bulk. In Raymond's book, hetero sex was too closely connected to blood and soil, brats and abortions, for someone who wasn't into the idea of progeny to get kicks from it. As these thoughts flashed through Ray's mind, a cold sweat filmed his skin. This girl's sexual needs, her widely spread legs, were sucking him deeper and deeper into a bottomless pit. There was no question about it, the pro-situ felt sick. Joyce was sapping his will, enveloping him within the vast empty spaces of her being.

Sebastian had left the room but quickly returned with a fresh tube of KY and some poppers. He handed the lubricant to Terry and lay flat on his stomach. Blake enjoyed rubbing the cool gel around his own fingers, across his palm and the back of his hand. Personally, Terry didn't go a bundle on S/M, although he'd always loved the sense of ritual that surrounded it. He placed the tube of KY against Sebastian's arse and discharged a considerable quantity of the lubricant. Blake's index finger penetrated the pro-situ's rim of dark pleasures, then he had two digits inside the arse. Without the KY, the rhythmic movement of Terry's hand would have caused a good deal of painful friction. The magic substance enabled Sebastian to ride this rising tempo as if it were an ever-growing ecstasy. He barely noticed as a third and then a fourth finger found their way into his posterior. As Blake forced his thumb into the shit-shute and formed his hand into a fist, the pro-situ's bowel muscles revolted and attempted to repel this invader with a series of spasmodic contractions.

'For Christ's sake, relax!' Terry cursed as he threw all his weight behind the fist. 'If you don't, you could end up with a serious injury.'

Sebastian reached out and grabbed a bottle of amyl nitrite. He inhaled the drug and was immediately overcome by a feeling of serenity. The muscle spasms ceased and Terry found himself elbow deep in the pro-situ's shit.

Sebastian was bellowing out his desires in a manner which led Blake to believe that this present humiliation was simply one of many which the sick bastard had brought down upon himself in a never-ending quest for kicks. Whatever the truth of the matter, few can deny there's a very thin dividing line between pleasure and pain. As a libertarian, Terry had no intention of preventing the pro-situ from indulging in whatever deviant acts turned him on – even if it meant the silly bugger ended up with piles and other personal hygiene problems.

'I wanted you to tear out my heart!' Sebastian exclaimed as Blake pulled his fist from the masochist's overstretched arsehole.

Then Sebastian fainted. Terry looked at his hand. It was coated with a mixture of shit and blood. The pro-situ's anal muscles had been pretty slack, so it was unlikely that this latest abuse had added much to the damage his sphincter had sustained over several years of thrill-seeking. Blake wandered through to the kitchen and washed at the sink. As he turned round, a packet of cornflakes caught his attention. Clean dishes and cutlery were lying on a draining-board, an unopened carton of milk had been stashed in the fridge. Terry poured himself a bowl of cereal. He was pissed off about his victim fainting on him and found the food very comforting.

'Terry,' Joyce screamed. 'Terry, come here this minute!'

'What is it now?' Blake protested as he stomped into the living-room with the bowl of cereal still in his hand.

'That bastard Sebastian's fallen asleep and I can't wake 'im up!' Joyce wailed. 'Ray doesn't get off on fuckin' me in the cunt and it shows in his performance. I thought the best remedy would be for 'im and 'is brother to do an American sandwich with Ray takin' me arse.'

'So what do you want me to do?' Terry demanded.

'Fill in for Sebastian,' Joyce replied.

'Oh, alright,' Terry said wearily, throwing what remained of his milk and cornflakes over Sebastian's face.

While traditionalists still swear by water, the sunshine breakfast proved to be exactly what Sebastian needed to bring his senses back into operation. He moaned and rolled on to his side. Blake hauled the dazed pro-situ to his feet and manoeuvred him to where Joyce and Raymond were lying on the carpet.

'There you go,' Terry announced triumphantly. 'I've woken 'im up. Now you get 'im to perform.'

'And what are you gonna do?' Joyce wanted to know.

'Watch you and wank,' Blake replied in a bored tone of voice.

The hippy, who by this time was lying on her side, slapped Sebastian around the face and was rather surprised to see his cock stiffen as a result. Raymond greased himself up and after rubbing some KY into Joyce's arse, slipped inside her. For a few seconds there was a painful friction. However, the lubricant soon worked its wonders and Ray's bloated love stick gave her no more grief.

The hippy grabbed Sebastian's plonker and pulled him inside her. Unfortunately, brothers don't always come good. The two boys moved sluggishly. Neither was much of a sexual athlete and Joyce knew that what she really needed for this scene were professionals of Terry's calibre.

Blake checked out the bookshelves and was disgusted by what he found. Apart from texts by Marx, Debord, Vaneigem and their ilk, it was all very middlebrow. A lot of English romanticism – Coleridge, De Quincey, Shelley. There were bales of surrealist garbage and several score of Picador paperbacks. Of the latter, the most distasteful to Terry were the so-called mass-market editions of novels by William S. Burroughs. Burroughs's outlaw status was as bogus as his avant-garde radicalism. It was easy for upper-class wankers to make a name for themselves in the arts. They had all the breaks – like the right education, family connections and no money problems to contend with before they 'made it'.

Terry snorted disdainfully when he caught sight of a copy of *A Clockwork Orange*, another overrated piece of shit. In his book, Richard Allen was a million times better than middlebrow nonsense that bandied (but never shamelessly exploited) so-called ultra-violence. In this household, the ravings of a half-witted schoolteacher were favoured over quintessential texts such as *Skinhead* and *Knuckle Girls*. These ex-public-school boys didn't own a single novel published by New English Library, they'd never read a word written by Mick Norman, Petra Christian or Guy N. Smith. They didn't have any Panther reprints of short stories by thirties' pulp masters like H.P. Lovecraft or Clark Ashton Smith. There were no biographies of mass murderers, none of the books ordinary people read and reread for pleasure. The novels stacked on the pro-situs' Habitat shelves all screamed breeding and taste!

Raymond and Sebastian were failing to set Joyce's soul alight. She was relieved when they removed their pricks from her bulk. She didn't need these sexual inadequates. What she wanted was a real man like Terry.

Arnold was still beating himself off in the downstairs toilet. He'd come four times in this single session and would turn it into an all-time personal record if he could only reach orgasm number five.

Rodney had wandered up to his bedroom and fallen asleep. Ray and Sebastian were crashed out on the living-room floor. Terry pulled a copy of *Elements of Refusal* by John Zerzan from a bookshelf, then walked through to the kitchen and dumped the paperback in a waste-disposal unit. It was a symbolic gesture. Zerzan was a particularly inept pro-situ theorist. Blake hoped that one day he'd wipe out the entire culture of pseudo-radicalism to which these ex-public-school boys subscribed. In the meantime he'd touch them for some dosh.

Three

'Of course I hate ethnics,' Brian Smith assured Inspector Stephens, 'but it was Reds not immigrants that done me over!'

'You've suffered concussion,' the inspector said kindly, 'and you're not thinking straight. Just relax and I'll tell you what happened.'

'It was me who was hospitalized!' Smith protested.

'As you walked down Sandringham Road,' the copper intoned, ignoring the fascist's interjection, 'you were abused and then chased by a gang of drug-crazed ethnics. They caught up with you outside Hackney Downs Station, beat you up and stole your wallet.'

'I've told you, Jim,' Brian said with a note of frustration creeping into his voice, 'a young white kid nicked my wallet after I crawled out of the phone-box. Commies did me over but they didn't steal anything.'

'Did you recognize the doctor who stitched you up?' Stephens demanded.

'No,' Smith replied. 'I was in too much pain to pay attention to anything like that.'

'He knew who you were.' There was more than a touch of sarcasm in Stephens's voice. 'It was Dr Donald Cohen!'

'The hard-line liberal and free-speech advocate?' Smith asked in disbelief.

'Yes,' Stephens hissed. 'He treated your injuries despite the fact that his name virtually topped the list of those traitors you claimed you wanted to hang when you were fighting the '79 election. Cohen told me that as a humanitarian he was morally obliged to patch you up.'

'What a wanker,' Smith sneered. 'If I'd known who he was, I'd have punched him on the nose.'

'I told him you'd admitted to me that it was on your orders that his car was smashed up and excrement shoved through his letter-box.'

'What did he say?' Smith demanded.

'That it had happened a long time ago and he'd learnt to forgive the racists.'

'Where's he living now? I'll send out the goon squad to harass him!'

'That's better – more like your old self,' Stephens said, brightening up. 'I was beginning to believe this Third Positionist nonsense had affected your thinking, What's the slogan you run under the mast-head of Cockney Nation?'

'Pride in our own kind, respect for others,' Smith pontificated.

'You've alienated a lot of people since you started peddling this new line,' the inspector informed him. 'You had the most support among my men when you headed the White Workers Party and contested the '79 election with your prophetic *Put the Ethnics in Work Camps to Make Them Earn Their Passage Home* platform.'

'But look what happened!' Smith wailed. 'Thatcher stole the patriotic vote by claiming she'd deal with the race problem. Of course she soon forgot her promises and, the next thing you knew, she was inviting three and a half million Chinese to come and settle in the country.'

'So why the hell did you drop your hard-line White Power stance?' the inspector demanded. 'Thatcher sold us all down the river, just like Ted Heath before her! If us patriots had stuck together, we wouldn't be witnessing the slow death of our beloved nation.'

'Once Thatcher got into power, we lost the financial support of the ultra-Tories,' Smith explained. 'And our White Workers Party splintered into several warring factions. I was expelled from the very organization I'd worked so hard at building into a fighting machine which could save Britain.'

'So what?' the copper hissed.

'This is a lean period,' the Third Positionist announced, 'a time that necessitates compromises so that we can rebuild the movement. Believe me, Jim, I'm a committed racist. It's my faith in the historic destiny of the British people and my desire to free them from the yoke of Zionism which gives me the strength to adopt this course of action. While some of my former comrades may claim I'm a traitor, I will one day prove them wrong. Just trust me, Jim, and be patient.'

'I'm gonna get you another cuppa,' the inspector said, 'and then I'll come back with an argument that'll make you change your mind about who done you over. These drug-peddling ethnics are corrupting our upstanding white youth with their degenerate habits. I need violent crimes which will give me the opportunity to sweep their filthy trade from the streets. These immigrants crawled out of the gutter, they know they're second rate. I can spit on them and they don't bat an eyelid. The only thing these subhumans care about is the profits from their pot sales. Once I've got an excuse to disrupt their livelihood, I'll force these parasites to fight back. The riots will quickly progress into a fully fledged race war. Our women, children and old folk will be afraid to walk the streets. Pressure from the public will force the government to arm the police. Then I'll receive orders to shoot blacks on sight. The ethnics will be forced to retreat into a few ghettos. We'll team up, my friend, the Mets and the White Workers. Mass police raids on Brixton and Notting Hill will become a national sport. We'll flush the immigrants out one at a time and hunt the bastards down like the wild animals we've always known them to be!'

The inspector went to fetch more tea, leaving Smith to ruminate over the prospects for genocide. The Third Positionist admired the inspector's racial pride but was frustrated by the copper's inability to appreciate the spiritual aspects of White Supremacy. The Teutonic race had brought civilization to the world. Only Aryan folk ways were worthy of being called culture. The task of repelling the tide that threatened to swamp the unique identity of the British people was a religious task or it was nothing! The barbarous superstitions and jungle rites that race-mixers had imported from the Third-World were a threat to the very concept of Aryan Brotherhood. The liberal do-gooders and their Zionist masters were cavorting in the muck of money-making. This decadence was a cancer eating away at the very soul of the Nordic nations. Too many whites valued an easy life over the unfolding of a divine plan. Westerners had become soft, they'd lost touch with the God-given inspiration that drove their forefathers to great achievement. Before a New Man could arise to sweep away the multiracial horde, Smith needed to find a way of inculcating the great mass of racists – such as Inspector Stephens – with religious conviction.

'Here's yer cuppa,' the policeman said. 'I'm gonna let you sit and drink your tea. When you've finished I want you to sign this statement.'

'What the hell's that?' the Third Positionist demanded as the inspector waved several sheets of paper at him.

'I told you,' the cop hissed, 'it's a statement saying you were brutally mugged by a bunch of drug-addled ethnics who chased you from Sandringham Road into Dalston Lane.'

'I'm not gonna sign it,' Smith insisted as he sipped his tea.

The inspector picked up his telephone and barked an order into it. He slammed down the receiver, pulled out his wallet and laid a tenner on his desk.

'Is that for me?' Smith asked hopefully.

'Of course not,' the cop fumed, 'it's for Arthur Roberts.'

'He's not here, is he?' the Third Positionist whispered anxiously.

'The bastard's on his way up,' Stephens said solemnly. 'Thanks to your stubbornness, he's just taken me for another ten quid. He's stung me for over a hundred already this year. My mates in Special Branch tell me he's never lost a bet. He was playing on my pride when he wagered I'd never persuade you to claim it was ethnics who beat you up. . . . Speak of the devil. Hey, you could knock!'

'Hello boys' was Arthur's opening gambit as he walked across the room and pocketed the tenner which the inspector had laid out for him.

Brian Smith gripped the arms of his chair. He didn't like anyone to know about the financial arrangements he'd made with Roberts. If it became general knowledge that the anti-fascist had funded his political activities for the past ten years, it would compromise Brian's moral authority. There was no doubt in Smith's mind that many supporters of the far-Right would turn against him if they heard so much as a whisper about how he financed his racial campaigns. While the Third Positionist assumed it was obvious to any impartial observer that he'd taken Roberts for a ride, there were plenty of bigots within the fascist movement who'd willingly believe the smears his enemies would inevitably make against him.

'Could . . . could . . . couldn't we discuss this alone?' Smith stammered.

'We're all friends here,' Roberts assured him. 'Jim and I have had our differences in the past but we're on a solid footing now. We've all got a vested interest in stirring up race riots. Anti-fascist fronts have been one of the Party's biggest recruitment ruses. Leninists can't afford to let the racist louts hang up their boots and retire. We need you and we're prepared to pay for your services. The police want civil strife so that they can pressurize Westminster into increasing the resources available for dealing with crime. You want race riots because you're a fascist bigot and they rally public support for the far-Right. However, the Left has always acquired the greatest gains in membership from the resulting political polarization. That's why I pay you to cause trouble. Personally, I feel sorry for the ordinary blacks, asians, jews and chinese, who suffer. But if your lot start getting really nasty, then they might just be baited into supporting my cause. I know about the inspector's modest funding of your activities, and he knows that without my support the fascist movement would have collapsed over the last ten years. Let's be frank with each other!'

'But what if word gets out that you've been funding me?' Smith demanded.

'It's such a ridiculous idea, no one would believe it,' Roberts assured him.

'Besides which,' Stephens put in, 'we all have a vested interest in keeping the information to ourselves.'

'Well said!' Roberts enthused as he slapped the inspector forcefully on the back.

'I suppose you want me to claim that I was mugged and viciously beaten by a gang of drug-addled blacks,' Smith said in a sulky tone.

'You're not just to say it,' Roberts pontificated, 'you're to believe it!'

'But this'll ruin the movement I've been building over the past three years!'

'Who gives a fuck?' Roberts swore. 'Everyone knows you're a racist bigot! This Third Positionist nonsense isn't doing any of us much good. I've gone along with the farce for too long. I think it's high time you returned to unabashed Nazism. That's what the public likes, it keeps recruits pouring into the anti-fascist movement and ultimately the Party. White Power provides us with the surest means of exploiting middle-class guilt, whereas your current apartheid line just doesn't cut it with our potential supporters.'

'I must protest,' Smith exploded. 'The Third Position is a viable alternative to capitalism and communism and has been put into practice in countries such as Libya, Ghana and Iran.'

36

'Come on,' Roberts said as he stifled a laugh, 'don't give me that bullshit. Save it for your recruits. I've got a file thicker than a telephone directory on you. I know for a fact that you're a Hitler fanatic. You've been peddling a historical revisionist line for years!'

'That was a grave error,' Smith assured his patron, 'and the comrades who still publish works on the so-called Holocaust are making a terrible mistake in confronting this small lie instead of the whole conspiracy! Let's face it, Hitler is a figment of the Jewish imagination and the Second World War never took place. Until 1939, the Cockney people had lived as so-called Edwardians for thousands of years. A single race, united by both blood and culture, had held the lands of Hackney, Tower Hamlets and Newham in trust for upwards of ten million years. Then the Zionist conspirators discovered a means of hypnotizing whole populations at a time. Through a systematic application of these mind-control techniques, they tampered with our racial memory and foisted a fabricated history upon a heroic White People. Cockney Nation is fighting for the very survival of its dear folk ways. If we lose our fight with the race-mixers, internationalism will prevail and our descendants will be branded non-kosher and turned into slaves by evil rabbis!'

Roberts had to hide his amusement at Smith's outburst. He'd never quite sussed the old fascist and still wondered whether the Third Positionist realistically expected him to believe these tall tales.

'I'm not anti-Semitic!' Smith bleated as Roberts insulted him yet again by suggesting he was a racist lout. 'I'm anti-Jewish!'

'Forget that,' his old sparring partner hissed. 'Let's get on with the matter in hand.'

'It's all very well for you,' the Third Positionist replied. 'It doesn't cost you anything if I claim I've been mugged by a gang of black youths. For me it means throwing away the three years I've spent building Cockney Nation into a viable political organization.'

'I wouldn't call it viable,' Roberts sneered. 'You've only got seven members.'

'Eight,' Smith corrected. 'Don't forget that I'm a member of the movement too! But you're missing the point with this numbers game. Despite the low membership, we exert an enormous influence on the youth of East London. Besides which, I have a mole working in Harold Denmark's organization. Give it a year or two and he'll split the group so that the entire London branch will come over to Cockney Nation.'

'If that happened today, you'd have a grand total of twenty-three followers,' Roberts chuckled.

'According to the last issue of your magazine, my movement has a membership of five hundred,' Smith reminded him.

'You can't believe everything you read in the papers,' Roberts mumbled.

'Yeah, particularly the *Probe*,' Smith sniggered.

'Don't take the piss,' Roberts snapped. 'I was spreading disinformation. You don't fuck with MI7, as you'll learn very quickly if you refuse to go along with our plans.'

'You can cut off my finance,' Smith retorted. 'I don't give a fuck! I'm a man of principles – I'll find another way to build the movement and fund our paper.'

'You really are very naïve,' Roberts laughed. 'Do you think you can walk out on me just like that, after accepting all the money I've put your way over the past ten years?'

'Fuck you!' Smith roared.

'Take this,' his controller replied, reaching into a pocket and removing several sheets of paper. 'It's a series of articles written to spearhead your campaign against drug abuse and simultaneously promote the Third Position. I've gone for a personal angle in places, using the savage mugging you received at the hands of toked-up Rastafarians to highlight the failure of the multicultural experiment. Repatriation will make everybody happy. The blacks can sit around on their banana plantations getting stoned without fear of arrest, while whites won't have to put up with what they view as criminal behaviour.'

'Don't mock me!' Smith cried, shaking his fist. 'I'll not put my name to your racist filth. Rastafarians don't want to be shipped back to Africa to laze around on banana plantations! They simply want the opportunity to return to their own lands, where they can pursue the traditions which have sustained them for more than one thousand generations.'

'What's this bullshit you're spouting?' Inspector Stephens demanded. 'Before Arthur came in you were calling them ethnics!'

'It's a Cockney Nation policy not to antagonize the police,'
Smith replied. 'However, I've come to the conclusion that it
was an error of judgement on my part to pander to your gutter
racism.'

'Fuck you!' Stephens snorted.

'He's been fucking all sorts of people,' Roberts said coldly as
he pulled a thick wad of photographs from a jacket pocket and
slapped them down on the inspector's desk.

Stephens stared in disbelief at the top photograph, which
showed Smith bent over a chair with a Rasta fucking him up
the arse. The picture underneath was of the Third Positionist
being fist-fucked by a Chinese youth. In the next he was being
sucked off by an Indian boy.

Smith lowered his head in shame. If these snaps were
circulated any further, it would be the end of his career on
the far-Right. He'd written several leaders in *Cockney Nation*
warning against weak morals and insisting that without the
correct spiritual orientation, Aryans exposed themselves to the
danger of being seduced into sexual experimentation with other
races. The penalty for interracial bonking was expulsion from
the movement and personal disgrace. Smith could see that he'd
been backed into a corner and so quietly accepted as fact the
story that he'd been viciously mugged by a gang of drug-crazed
blacks.

'You . . . you. . . . You're a race-mixing queer,' Stephens
stammered. 'How could you?'

'It's hard to live up to the high ideals we set for ourselves,'
Smith admitted sadly. 'Let me show you how easy it is to
descend to the depths of sheer animal lust. . . .'

Smith got on his knees. He put his hand on the cop's fly
and pulled down the zip. Stephens's face turned bright red
as his love muscle hardened in the fascist's palm. He'd had
the fantasies since boyhood, but until today they'd never got
beyond the stage of wet dreams and the occasional wank over
a body culture magazine.

The inspector gasped with pleasure as Smith licked the tip of
his meat while working its base with his hand. The primitive
rhythm activated a million-year-old genetic code buried at
the very centre of the cop's brain. Stephens was no longer
a participant in the twentieth century. He'd returned to that
period when the curtain of history first rose upon his native land.

He was gratified to find that the racial stock which subsisted on these islands in this pagan era was the blood kin of those who still inhabit the mighty British nation. Yes, even then, the English could be distinguished as belonging to the Nordic breed of the European race. This was a heroic people who, when they saw an arse, a cunt or a mouth, just had to fill these holes with wads and wads of come. A people unafraid to spill their genetic juice, the very future of their race, into any orifice they had the opportunity to plumb. A people destined to conquer the world!

The cop was being worked up and down the scales of ecstasy and it sure as hell beat making it with the wife! He knew now that the way forward for his country was a return to its traditional values of rape, pillage and plunder.

'God, Queen and Country!' Stephens screamed as he prepared to spill the very life-blood of his race.

The inspector experienced orgasm as a tidal wave of patriotism. Sickened by race traitors and democrats of every stripe, the White Folk of London stormed Parliament and installed a National Socialist government. The mass repatriation of non-whites began immediately and was swiftly followed by the extermination of Marxists, atheists, liberal toadies and all other socially undesirable elements. After six months of frenzied activity, the population was reduced to somewhere around fourteen thousand – a hard-core Nordic gene pool from which the Master Race would be reborn!

Realizing that the inspector was regaining his grip on what was going on around him, Arthur Roberts slipped an auto-focus camera back into his bag.

Brian Smith swallowed the love juice that had been discharged into his throat and then pushed the cop over a regulation police desk. Roberts pulled a tube of KY from his bag and tossed it to the Third Positionist. The Führer of Cockney Nation smeared the gel into the inspector's arse and then proceeded to rub it all over his own cock.

In the meantime, London's leading anti-fascist had dropped his trousers and inserted his love muscle into the cop's mouth. Stephens was gagging on the fucking thing! He liked the taste but was afraid he was going to choke. Jim tried to place his hand around the base of Arthur's dick but the top pushed it away. Then, with a thrust of his pelvis, Roberts forced his fuck stick into the policeman's throat.

'You'd never make it as a mason,' the anti-fascist laughed as Stephens went blue in the face. 'You have to go through a lot worse than this just to get admitted!'

Smith held his love pole against the copper's arse and thrust forward. The inspector coughed and nearly bit off his other playmate's cock as the Third Positionist's rod penetrated the rim of dark pleasures. Stephens no longer knew whether he was experiencing pleasure or pain as a mass of undifferentiated sensation brought a flood of endorphins into his brain. The hard-line cop was no longer able to distinguish between the prick that had been forced down his throat and the love stick beating out a primitive signature in his arse. All that mattered was to keep up with the beat, to feel the blood and endorphins being pumped through his cortex at an incredible rate. If Stephens had been in possession of his critical faculties, he'd have denounced this steamy session as having been compromised by degenerate negroid rhythms. However, in his sexed-up state, he hadn't even noticed Roberts activating a cassette player or the fact that his group-fuck buddies were now moving their bodies to a hypnotic blues beat.

'Listen to me,' Roberts was saying as he moved his cock in and out of the inspector's throat. 'Listen to me, tune in to my voice. I want you to go with the flow, relax, let your body move naturally and concentrate on this message.'

Smith was grinning. He was pumping himself up towards orgasm, feeling certain that this sex session was turning the cop on to the spiritual values which act as the guiding principles of the Great White Race. Sex, the Third Positionist reflected, was central to the continued expansion and development of his people. They had to be made to breed, to increase their numbers. This was the only way to counteract the threat they faced from the alien hordes who for the time being enjoyed a far higher birth rate. It didn't matter what sort of fucking Aryans invoked in their bid to become sexpots. Gay was as good as straight. Even interracial sex was permissible if it didn't result in procreation. The fact was, the more sex you had, the more you wanted, and if whites had more sex, then the birth rate of this chosen people would eventually climb. Whatever happened, racial suicide in the form of abortion and the pill had to stop.

'As we plan the future race riots together' – Roberts was using his most authoritarian tone of voice – 'you'll lose confidence in your own abilities. You'll accept my natural leadership qualities and come to rely on my judgments. . . .'

The inspector was totally absorbed in the anti-fascist's fantasy. He was floating on a sea of pleasure, but a tidal wave of sensation threatened to drown him if for one instant his attention wandered from the words being uttered by that all-powerful source of wisdom. The speech was being inscribed whole in the furthermost depths of his cortex, bypassing any conscious evaluation of its content on Stephens's part.

'I'm gonna switch off the tape,' Roberts was saying, 'and then Smith and I will shoot our loads. You'll experience orgasm as a rapid promotion to the rank of commander-in-chief, then wake up from this sexual sleep forgetting everything I've told you. But you'll act on my commands and look forward to getting your arse fucked again.'

The anti-fascist reached into his bag and killed the music with which he'd brainwashed the other two men. He and Smith came simultaneously and the whole thing turned into a tidal wave of an orgasm which washed through three separate but intimately linked bulks. To Roberts, the feeling was akin to printing a smear in *Anti-Fascist Probe* which totally discredited the British anarchist and Trotskyite movements, thereby leaving the way clear for hard-line Stalinists to clean up on the Left.

'Right,' Roberts said as he dried himself with a Kleenex from a box on the inspector's desk, 'we'll meet up again tomorrow.'

'Sure,' Smith replied as he pulled up his trousers.

'Can you manage that, Jim?' the anti-fascist wanted to know.

'Yes,' the inspector assured him.

As Smith and Roberts had adjusted their clothing, the policeman decided he'd better follow suit. He wasn't sure how one was supposed to behave after group sex with two other men.

'OK,' Roberts said in a businesslike manner, 'let's make it one o'clock. We can have a spot of lunch together.'

'We'll soon have the ethnics rioting,' the cop said as he nodded his head in approval of both the suggested time and the idea of food.

'Suits me,' Smith replied without enthusiasm.

'Great, it's all settled,' the anti-fascist concluded with a grin.

Then without warning Stephens burst into song. 'England arise! the long, long night is over.' The inspector's voice swelled as a tidal wave of post-coital ecstasy swept over him.

'Faint in the east behold the dawn appear,' Smith joined in.
'Come on!' the cop urged his anti-fascist chum.
'Out of the evil dream of toil and sorrow.' Roberts fished his cock out of his flies as he added his voice to their rendition of Edward Carpenter's anthem.

The editor of the *Probe* was of the heartfelt opinion that patriotic crap was a waste of time. The only reason he went along with the singsong was to keep the other two happy.

'Arise, O England, for the day is here!' The anti-fascist struggled to remember the words as he beat his meat. His two comrades had followed his lead and now had their plonkers in their hands.

> 'From your fields and hills,
> Hark! the answer swells:
> Arise O England, for the day is here!'

The three men stood in the sparsely furnished office exploring the delights of auto-sexuality and simultaneously giving voice to their country's ancient tradition of rabid nationalism.

> 'People of England all your valleys call you,
> High in the rising sun the lark sings clear:
> Will you dream on, let the shameful slumber thrall you?
> Will you disown your native land so dear?
> Shall it die unheard,
> That sweet pleading word?
> Arise, O England, for the day is here!'

The men's movements were becoming wilder. Their voices were less steady than when they'd sung the opening bars of this clarion call for imperialism and bigotry. Brian Smith was dreaming of the night rallies he'd organize once he'd overthrown Britain's democratic government.

> 'Forth then, ye heroes, patriots and lovers,
> Comrades of danger, poverty and scorn,
> Mighty in faith of freedom, your great mother,
> Giants refreshed in joy's new rising morn!
> Come swell the song,
> Silent now so long . . .'

Roberts shot off a wad of his genetic wealth and the liquid DNA spurted into the inspector's left eye. This so excited the policeman that he let fly with his own seed, which with a fearsome splat hit the ceiling and then dripped to the floor. Smith took careful aim and a jet of his love juice found its way into the copper's mouth. As a result, Stephens had trouble mouthing the final line of Carpenter's song: 'England is risen! And the day is here!'

Four

Terry tried to orientate himself. He'd woken up in Habitatland. He was lying on a double futon with a girl and another boy. The sunlight streaming between the partly drawn curtains hurt his eyes.

'Ooooh, Christ,' Blake groaned.

He'd worn himself out by spending most of the previous night screwing. Now he was suffering from both excess physical exertion and a severe lack of sleep. Who the fuck was the boy lying next to him? Terry racked his brain and eventually drew forth the name Arnold Chance. The bashful pro-situ's mates had turned him into the butt-end of their jokes because he'd not taken part in the orgy. Chance had kept himself locked in the downstairs toilet all evening and through most of the night. Raymond had told Joyce and Terry they might as well use Arnold's bed, as he didn't seem to want it for himself. Chance had crawled beneath his duvet after the two guests had fallen asleep. That was why Terry had been so disorientated when he woke up – there'd been an extra body lying next to him.

Terry turned over and his movements woke Joyce. Her eyelids fluttered and then opened wide. The hippy smiled and Blake could feel the Cheshire cat grin on his own face as he gazed into her eyes. Joyce put her arms around Terry's shoulders and brought her face close to his. Their lips met and the hippy opened Blake's mouth with her tongue. Joyce could feel Terry's cock hardening against her. She trawled a hand down his side and squeezed the love muscle. Blake's breathing quickened, Joyce had taken him ten times the previous night and was unashamedly demanding to have him again. She rubbed her fingers over his balls and then, in a single movement, ran them along the length of his cock.

Terry could feel the hardness in the hippy's nipples as she pressed herself against him. She was running her tongue around his cracked lips. The pressure of her body forced him on to his back and, as he tumbled, he clipped Arnold's arm with his shoulder. The pro-situ woke, jumped out of bed and bolted from the room. Blake thought he was going to suffocate as

Joyce pressed her mouth against his lips, thereby stifling his laughter.

The hippy was forcing more and more of her tongue into Terry's mouth and simultaneously using her hand to work his length. She swung a leg over him and guided his love muscle into her hot, creamy slit. Joyce was wet with desire and Blake slid into the inner mystery of her being. He let the hippy set a cracking pace. As they pumped up the volume, Terry imagined that he was Karl Marx, making it with the servant girl while his wife Jenny looked on.

Joyce had left Hackney. Indeed, she'd left her native country behind. She was reliving an earlier life in which she'd been an Indian squaw. The braves she'd known then were no different to the men she knew now. They'd all thought she was an empty hole and wanted to fill her, never realizing that she couldn't be filled. Men were incapable of giving her enough of what she demanded. But Joyce was a nympho with a difference – she didn't think of her sex partners as sluts, slags or slaves to their dicks. As far as she was concerned, there was no reason why freely consenting adults should be subject to abuse for giving expression to their sexual desires.

Terry was no longer thinking about Red Jenny. He'd decided he didn't need communist fantasies to act as a barrier between himself and reality. Marx, who was fundamentally an aesthete, had used Capital to mediate between himself and the Other – the concept of alienation had enabled him to withdraw from the world. Rather than attempt to overcome his chronic shyness and lack of social grace, the lawyer's son had excused his bumbling manner on the grounds that the economy was an imposition between I and Thou.

Blake knew there was no economic base that determined a cultural and political superstructure. Such beliefs were simply an abdication of responsibility on the part of middle-class Bohemians. Wo/man had created the economy, and as soon as s/he ceased to reproduce it, the economy would disappear. Lefties used the base/superstructure fantasy as a means of protecting themselves from the harsh realities of this world. Politics is a clash of wills. While Marxists refuse to admit this, their vociferousness in attacking any individual who contradicts their ludicrous orthodoxy demonstrates that they're still forced to act on such facts in order to make headway against their political opponents.

Terry was a boot-boy, a skinhead, a working-class warrior who was ready and able to take on all those who would oppress him with their determinist doctrines. Marxists were no different from liberal–conservatives – both believed society was ordered via the mechanisms of the economy. Worse still were the gene-fixated fascists who insisted that an individual's racial origins determined her destiny – these wankers refused to accept that wo/man could remake herself as she pleased and that all limits were self-imposed.

Joyce was working herself up and down Terry's cock. She'd known him less than twenty-four hours but was already well aware that he liked to hold off on his orgasm just to demonstrate the high level of control he exercised over all his bodily functions. Joyce was determined to bring him off quickly. She rocked harder and faster, piled on the pressure. Blake lay moaning beneath her. The sexual stimulation had activated a genetic code buried at the very centre of his cortex.

Arnold was in the bathroom with his plonker in his hand. He was fantasizing about the night he'd just spent in bed with a woman. He was imagining what it would have been like if he'd been lying next to Joyce instead of Terry. The pro-situ pinched his nipples. He wanted the hippy to suck his cock. It would take a lot of rationalizing before he'd build up the courage to put it in her cunt.

'Goats and monkeys!' Blake barked as he shot off a wad of liquid genetics.

'Gotcha,' Joyce hissed in ecstasy.

She liked the way it felt when a bloke came inside her and she'd proved her point. Despite Terry's obsession with control, she'd decided when he filled her up, it was her womanly skills which had brought forth copious flows of his love juice! And now she was wondering whether Blake had put her in the club and, if he had, how he'd take to his responsibilities as a father.

Terry had sunk back into the pillows and was going through the angles for getting dosh out of the well-heeled pro-situs whose hospitality he was enjoying. He'd explored the house the previous evening and the whole place shouted money. Pleasant dreams flooded his mind as Joyce stroked the quarter-inch of bristle that stood up from his scalp.

'I've never fucked a skinhead before,' Joyce was saying. 'I've always thought they looked ugly. But there's something about you. Your hair feels really nice . . .'

Blake ignored her comments. He was systematically reviewing every snippet of conversation the pro-situs had uttered in his presence. They seemed to be down on ecology, if he could only come up with some theory and the right proposition! Talking to them a bit more would help him sort out his ideas. He decided to pursue the possibilities over breakfast.

'Time to get up!' Terry barked at Joyce as he leapt out of bed.

'But it's only five past eight!' she protested.

'That's late,' Blake retorted. 'I'm not some hippy layabout, you know. I usually get up before eight.'

'Get back into bed and relax,' Joyce whispered.

'No way,' Terry replied as he whipped the duvet off the bed. 'There's only so many shopping hours in the day and you'll waste half of them if you lie in your pit all morning!'

'I'm gonna stick with laid-back hippy boys in future!' Joyce snapped as she conceded defeat by getting up from the futon.

Fortunately, Arnold had vacated the bathroom by the time Terry wanted to wash. The skinhead grinned as he spotted the globules of spunk around the toilet, firm evidence that the pro-situ had enjoyed a wild, if somewhat furtive, wank. Blake pissed and then proceeded to wash his hands, face, prick and underneath his arms. Joyce came in as he was searching around for an unused toothbrush. He found one in the medicine cabinet. As he was undoing the Cellophane wrapping, the hippy picked up a bottle of deodorant and wiped it under her left arm.

'Hey,' Terry shouted, 'you should wash yourself before you do that!'

'Wimmin don't need to,' Joyce replied. 'They don't sweat the way men do.'

'You dirty little hippy,' Blake shot back. 'Everyone should wash under their arms in the morning. It's basic personal hygiene.'

As Terry said this he grabbed hold of Joyce and manoeuvred her over to the wash-basin. He lifted up and splashed water underneath first one and then the other of her arms. Blake lathered up some soap and applied the suds to the erogenous zones in question, before rinsing these away with warm water. Having completed the operation to his own satisfaction, he took the deodorant from Joyce's hand and applied it to her cleansed skin. 'Now wash your cunt,' Terry ordered.

Not wishing to provoke the working-class warrior's wrath any further, Joyce obeyed. Blake picked up the toothbrush and removed what remained of its packaging. As he did so, he fantasized that Andrea Dworkin had been driven to polemic by his behaviour. Terry imagined this radical feminist seizing upon it as further proof of her claim that men view woman as filth.

As a skinhead, Terry was justly proud of his severe appearance. To the bourgeoisie, his cropped hair made him featureless and thus less than an individual. In a sense, this rendered him anonymous and invisible. To uptight careerists he was merely a speck among the faceless horde who threatened the very stability of consumer society. A lot of yuppie bastards were sexually attracted to Blake because he posed a threat to the world order they supported. Terry's appearance aroused moral indignation, which led innumerable trendies to fantasize about possessing him. They wanted to fuck, and be fucked, by someone who rejected plastic individualism. They wanted to feel Blake sliding in and out of their hot slits and arse-holes.

Joyce had completed her ablutions. Terry positioned himself in front of the basin so that he could clean his teeth. When he'd finished, he handed the toothbrush to the hippy and marched back to Arnold's bedroom. He lovingly fingered his sta-pres before slipping into them. Then pulled on his Ben Sherman and fastened the buttons with fetishistic devotion. He considered dressing the most important ritual of the day.

Joyce came into the room and pulled on her gear without any sense of decorum. When Terry'd finished lacing up his DMs, the pair of them went down to the kitchen.

'Did you get your clothes while we were both in the bathroom?' Joyce asked Arnold who was standing over the cooker, frying bacon.

'Yeah,' the pro-situ mumbled in an embarrassed tone.

'Never mind that,' Terry put in, 'what's for breakfast?'

'There's cornflakes,' Chance replied, 'or you can have bacon and eggs, or toast, or muesli, or porridge, or beans. I've just made some coffee.'

Terry filled two mugs with java. He was relieved the pro-situs had filtered because he couldn't abide the instant variety. He found some milk and sloshed it into the coffee. Joyce picked up one of the mugs and sipped at the brew while Blake lifted two bowls from the draining-board and proceeded to search for spoons.

'The drawer to your left,' Arnold said helpfully.

'Thanks,' Terry whispered.

Joyce was thinking about the future as Blake poured corn-flakes into her bowl and added milk. She was sick of being single and thoroughly disillusioned with the life she'd been leading. She was happy enough with the hippy front, it was what lay beneath it that chewed her up. She wanted a baby, wanted to settle down and raise a family. Terry would make the ideal husband. He'd a strong body and a sharp mind, qualities that would be passed on to their children. Joyce considered Blake's subversive posturing to be a passing fad. He struck her as a clever businessman who used revolutionary rhetoric as a means of striking deals and selling products. Joyce knew more about Terry than he was ever likely to suspect. As far as she could see, his real interests were intimately linked to a harmless obsession with sex and pornography.

'So tell me about Dawson-Rand,' Blake said to Arnold as the pro-situ sat down at the table with them. 'Where does his money come from and how often does he get laid?'

'Rupert', Chance replied, 'is a kleptomaniac. He goes on endless shop-lifting sprees. He mainly works bookshops. What he does is beat up his spoils so that they look second-hand. He then sells them from a stall in Camden Market. He makes a good living because he specializes in material which will appeal to lefties with plenty of dosh.'

'How much does he earn a week?' Terry wanted to know.

'Anything up to seven or eight hundred quid. Like I said, he's a kleptomaniac and he has a big turnover.'

'What about the birds, then?' The skinhead grinned.

'Oh, I don't know,' the bashful pro-situ replied, 'but he must have a lot of sex because he goes to the clap clinic once a month for a check-up!'

'Sounds like my kind of man,' Blake said, slapping a thigh. 'And what about his politics? Does he recognize the necessity of speeding up the evolutionary process? Has he taken a clear stand against ecology?'

'Not only Rupert but all of My One Flesh are totally opposed to ecology,' Arnold informed him proudly. 'We've repeatedly

50

denounced the Greens as the ideological agents of Capital. Only a middle-class wanker could whine on about the state of the world when it's quite clear that the crucial issue is the lot of the workers.'

'So you all understand that ecological destruction plays a vital role in the historical development of the workers' movement? Not only are the workers going to overthrow the bourgeoisie, they'll simultaneously mutate through the effects of radiation and other allegedly poisonous fall-out. The institution of communism will be accompanied by wo/man's transformation into a new physical being.'

'I don't think we've ever discussed that,' Chance admitted, rather at a loss about how to deal with this novel item which had found its way on to Blake's political agenda.

'But you can see my point,' Terry hissed. 'That if you're against the middle classes wanking off over ecological politics, then you have to view the workers' revolution as a nuclear evolution.'

'I . . . I . . . I suppose so,' the pro-situ stammered, 'although I don't think Debord ever wrote anything to that effect.'

'But you've read his *Commentaries on the Society of the Spectacle?*'

'Of course!' the pro-situ retorted, deeply offended that anyone would even suggest that he hadn't read all of the great man's works.

'Well,' Terry continued, 'you know that Debord wasn't at liberty to speak freely because the agents of repression study everything he writes. You know all about the decoys in the book to confuse ideologues of every stripe.'

'Yes, yes!' Arnold shouted angrily. 'I know all of that.'

'But you obviously didn't realize that the book was also secretly coded,' the skinhead said triumphantly.

Arnold admitted defeat by slumping in his chair. Debord was fiendishly clever. Only a genius could have predicted prior to the slumps of the seventies that Capital had overcome its internal contradictions. It didn't become clear until after the latter period of economic turbulence that what Debord said was true not of the sixties (when he'd first advanced the claim) but of the nineteen nineties. Chance felt he should have guessed that, as well as containing decoys, Debord's texts were brim full of secret messages.

Terry couldn't believe his luck. This theoretical jerk-off artist had fallen for his outrageous lies. He wondered what Debord would make of the claim that his texts contained secret messages – perhaps he'd assert that it was true! Regardless of this, one thing was certain – the Situationist leader was unlikely to agree with the skinhead's interpretation of his work. But to return to pro-situs, having swallowed the ruse about secret messages, Arnold would accept any political line Blake cared to peddle. If the other members of My One Flesh were as gullible as Arnold, Terry'd soon have the group buying up some very expensive nuclear weapons. He'd sell them an assortment of missiles which didn't even exist!

'So when do the others get up?' Blake wanted to know.

'About one,' Chance replied.

'Lunch-time!' the skinhead exclaimed in horror.

'It's not lunch-time if you've only just got up,' Arnold replied in their defence.

'Bohemians! Fuckin' Bohemians!' Blake shouted in dismay.

'We're not!' the pro-situ insisted in an offended tone of voice. 'We're theoretically coherent situationist revolutionaries.'

'Look,' Terry said as he stood up and grabbed Joyce by the arm, 'I've not got time to hang around here waiting for your mates to catch up on their beauty sleep. I'll come around later this week and we can all have a serious political discussion.'

'OK.' Chance yawned.

'See you later,' Blake hissed as he pulled Joyce down the hall.

'I'm going back to bed,' the pro-situ said defiantly.

Terry ignored the remark and marched to Hackney Central Station with Joyce trailing along behind him. They hit the platform as an east-bound train pulled in. Joyce sat down opposite Blake, kicked off her sneakers and proceeded to massage his balls and fuck stick with the soles of her feet.

Terry'd always loved being felt up, but Joyce was the first person to do it so openly – and with her feet! A middle-aged woman sitting on the opposite side of the carriage glared disapprovingly before burying her head in a Mills and Boon romance. Blake, who was as stiff as hell, was wondering if this jumbo erection would burst the seams of his briefs.

When they pulled in at Homerton, Joyce had to lower her legs for a few seconds to let an underdressed blonde get on the train. Smiling at Joyce, she sat down next to Terry. Feeling the hippy's

52

feet return to their resting-place on his crotch, Blake felt even hornier than before. The woman who'd sat next to him laid a notepad on her lap and proceeded to scribble across it at a frantic speed. Terry glanced down at the letter she was writing:

Dear Steve, it's your wife. I just thought I would write and let you know how I am getting on, and what you are about to read will no doubt shock you. Well Steve, as you know, I was a virgin when we were married. I remember our wedding night; watching you taking off your clothes, and when you dropped your pants, and I saw your big fat cock, I was shaking with excitement knowing that you were going to ram it right up my hot wet fanny. Do you remember that you came into bed, took my hand and placed it around your huge prick and told me to wank you off? And I didn't know how to do it, until you showed me.

Terry eyed the girl up. She was somewhere between twenty and twenty-five. Her dress with its plunging neckline had been too tight a year ago. Her bleached hair and three-inch heels were a sexual invitation. The blonde smiled without looking up as she realized Blake was appraising her. Joyce applied enough extra pressure to Terry's balls to make him wince, but this didn't deter the boot-boy from following the course of the woman's spidery handwriting:

Well Steve, there's nothing I don't know now, you taught me quite a lot in the two short years we were married. Do you remember when I came home from work and caught you shagging the arse off that little fat cow Jane? It's been over a year now and believe me, Steve, I've learnt a great deal. In the last year I HAVE BEEN FUCKED STUPID. Eight different men have been up me, including a big black man. My could he shag, and what a cock, it was a whopper, bigger and thicker than yours. I'll tell you about him and all the other antics I've been up to since I left you and came here to London.

Terry was beginning to understand the bird's attraction. She was obviously a fruit-cake. He'd always gone for girls who were mildly psychotic. The type of mental sickness that attracted him usually manifested itself bodily in a skinny physique. The blonde was actually of medium build but obviously well gone in the head. She was certainly getting off on the fact that Blake was reading every word of this epistle to her husband:

I have a flat here in the East End. One night I was sitting up feeling a bit lonely when there was a knock on the door. When I answered it I was greeted by Derek from upstairs. He wanted change for the meter. He is twenty-five and what a body. Once when he was going up the stairs in front of me my fanny became dripping wet just from watching the way he moved his lovely firm bum. I imagined what it would be like lying naked with him, fingering his arse, touching his big black cock, cupping his hairy balls in my hands. That night I found out. When he saw I was alone, he suggested I go and get a carry-out and that we keep each other company. Having glanced between his legs and seen the shape of his cock pressed against his tight jeans, I decided to accept this offer. He said he would be about half an hour. I took a shower, put on my skin-tight white slacks. As you know, Steve, I have a lovely tight bum, and I was making sure he'd see every crack I had.

The train pulled in at Hackney Wick and Joyce had to lower her legs to let the woman who'd given them the filthy glare get past. The old biddy got out, slamming the door as the hippy returned her feet to their resting-place against Terry's crotch. The skinhead was getting really steamed up. The combination of his girl's ministrations and the kinky antics of the blonde made him ache for a fuck. He looked up, smiled lecherously at Joyce and then focused his gaze on the divorcee's notepad:

He came back, we had a few drinks. When I bent down to clean the ash-tray, he said 'I hope you don't mind Donna but you have the loveliest bum I have ever seen.' I told him not to be naughty but when I was putting the ash-tray back I felt his hands sizing up my arse. He was really giving it a good feel. He asked if I was liking it. I told him that it was nice but it would be much better if I took my pants off. He said 'Good.' I said 'Do you want to screw me?' 'What do you think?' he said, rubbing at his cock. I looked down and saw he had a big hard-on.

'What are you doing this afternoon?' Joyce asked.
'I gotta work on some video,' Terry replied without looking up.

Without saying a word, I knelt down in front of Derek and started feeling his cock. Ten seconds later we were both naked. When I saw his big thick prick I almost fainted. What a size it was! I held his cock in my hand and pumped it up and down. Then I leant over and took his big blunt knob in my mouth and started sucking it. By this time my fanny was soaking wet, desperate for his cock. I couldn't help it, I started to whisper to him to stick it up me. 'Please give me it,' 'I want it,' 'Shag me,' I was saying. He said 'You really are desperate for it, aren't you, hot arse!'

Terry reflected that Donna wasn't the only one desperate for a fuck. He was aching to get a mouth, arse, hand or cunt around his throbbing member. He wanted to screw both Joyce and this blonde there and then on the train.

He said he would fuck my brains out but first I must do things for him. I told him I would do anything he wanted. He said that he could think of a lot of filthy things, some of them really perverted. I said I didn't care. 'OK,' he said, 'lick my balls.' I started licking his big balls. He lifted his legs up to his chest and said 'Can you see my arse-hole?' I said 'Yes.' 'Then put your lovely soft lips right on it and kiss it.' Yes, Steve, your hot arse wife put her mouth on his hole and rimmed it.

Joyce increased the pressure on Terry's balls until he was audibly panting. Then, without warning, she removed her feet and put on her sneakers.

He was moaning and groaning with pleasure. He put his hands on my behind, pulled my cheeks apart and I felt his finger go up my arse-hole. I was that hot I started moving my bum up and down with his finger. He said 'You like that, don't you!' I loved it. Then he said 'How would you like me to put my cock up your bum-hole?' I said it would be sore because of the size of his prick. He said that if I put cream on my hole it would just slip up me. I was so hot I said yes. I bent down in front of him. I felt the cream on my hole. It was nice and cool. Then he got round the back of my arse. I felt his big cock between my bum cheeks . . .

'Come on, bozo,' Joyce said, pulling Terry up from his seat, 'Stratford.'

As he got out of the carriage, the skinhead felt the blonde slide a chit of paper into the back pocket of his sta-pres. He didn't need to look at it to know it was her phone number. Blake smiled at her as he closed the carriage door, then ran after Joyce and grabbed hold of her from behind.

'Leave it out!' the hippy screamed as he rubbed his crotch against her arse.

'What's the matter with you?' Terry demanded.

'You was eyeing up that bird on the train,' Joyce said. 'Don't deny it, I saw you.'

'So what?' the skinhead replied. 'I only met you yesterday. Besides, I didn't complain when you wanted a line-up.'

'I don't care who you fuck when I'm not around,' Joyce spat, 'as long as when I'm playing with your bits you give me all your attention.'

'I'm sorry,' Terry replied lamely.

They walked in silence to the platform from which the Docklands Light Railway departed. An electronic display informed them that a train would pull into the terminus in three minutes. Terry put his arms around Joyce and she let him slip his tongue inside her mouth. The hippy liked the way the boot-boy pressed himself against her body. She wanted him now and forever. Having always sworn she'd settle down before she was thirty, Joyce knew instinctively that Blake was the right man for her. All she had to do was tame him. He'd make the ideal father for her baby.

'Come on,' Terry said, pulling Joyce along by the hand.

The train had pulled in and was disgorging its dozen passengers. Blake loved sitting at the front of these driverless models. He wasn't going to let anyone spoil his day by occupying the best seats before him.

'Hey,' Joyce shouted as Terry pulled her down next to him, 'you still haven't given me your phone number.'

'Aren't you coming home with me?' the skinhead demanded as he handed Joyce one of his cards.

'I've got to make a cake for me mum's birthday,' the hippy lied.

Joyce was worried that if she appeared too easy, Terry would lose interest in her. She'd always believed that the way to a man's heart was by playing hard to get. The hippy liked the way Blake's mouth met hers, liked the way he was massaging her tit. She knew she'd got him well steamed up and figured that, by denying him sex now, she'd demonstrate herself as worthy of serious attention.

'Bow Church,' Joyce said, getting up and kissing Terry on the top of his head. 'See you later.'

'Bollocks,' Blake swore. 'Trust her to live just one stop from Stratford!'

He watched Joyce step on to the platform and walk towards the exit. The automatic doors whooshed shut and the train chugged out of the station. Terry felt in dire need of sexual release and so made a careful appraisal of the situation. The only decent-looking woman he could see was wearing the blue uniform of a Light Railway employee. Blake didn't go for the gear but liked the slim build and long black hair. He smiled at the girl. She ignored him and busied herself checking tickets.

A passable brunette got on at Devons Road but she was with her husband and two kids. Terry reckoned that if she'd been on her own he could have picked her up in ten seconds flat. He continued to focus his attention on the guard. His first breakthrough came as the train pulled out of Poplar. The girl smiled at him! Blake felt a wave of elation surge through his bulk. He really fancied this chick!

As the train pulled in and out of several more stops and guard duties kept the woman away from him, Terry got increasingly restive. It was only after they chugged out of Mudchute that she finally came and sat next to him.

'Did you stay on after your stop?' she asked in soft, feminine tones.

'Yeah,' Terry replied.

'Then I guess you deserve me number.'

She wrote the name INDRA in block capitals and then centred the all-important digits underneath.

'I don't drink but I like dancing and going to the cinema,' Indra told Terry as she handed him her details.

'That's great,' he told her. 'I don't drink or smoke and I'm a vegetarian too.'

'Snap!' came the reply and then, after a moment's hesitation, 'Your gear gives a different impression, you look like a trouble-maker. That's why I wasn't sure whether or not I should speak to you. After a while I decided you couldn't be a racist, 'coz no bigot would be so upfront about wanting to chat me up. Sometimes it's a problem being Indian and going for boot-boys, I 'ave to be very thorough sussing blokes out. I've got really good at it. Most of the geezers I pick up turn out to be in Skinheads against Racial Prejudice.'

The train pulled into Island Gardens. Indra got up and pressed the button which opened the automatic doors.

'I'll give you a ring,' Terry told her as he stepped on to the platform.

'You do that,' she replied.

Blake decided he might as well walk home. As he was leaving the station, a girl bumped into him. She bent down, picked up a scrap of card and gave it to the skinhead.

'You dropped this,' she said in a thick German accent before hurrying up the stairs to the trains.

Terry examined the card. Printed on one side was the information *Artcore Gallery, Weisestrasse 58, Berlin 44. 6227359.* Handwritten on the reverse was the name *Birgit* and a London telephone number. Terry slipped the chit into the back pocket of his sta-pres.

As he strode along, the skinhead had a thousand and one dirty thoughts. It wasn't long before the familiar shape of Kelson House loomed before him. A bleached blonde in her early twenties was waiting for the lift.

'What number?' she asked Terry as they got in.

'Twenty-third,' he replied and then added, 'Do you live here?'

'No,' the blonde simpered. 'I'm just visiting me sister.'

'This place is a fuckin' shit-hole,' the skinhead informed her. 'Half the flats are infested. The locals call it Cockroach City.'

'I know,' the girl informed him. 'Me sister's been living here five years.'

'Do ya come here often?' Blake wanted to know.

'Yeah, every week.'

'I'm Terry. You can come and see me in two hundred and ten if you're ever looking for something different to do.'

'I'll bear it in mind,' the blonde told him as she got out of the lift.

The doors clanked shut and Blake was whooshed up another ten floors. He resisted the urge to wank as soon as he got into his flat. The skinhead figured some music would give direction to the sexual tension that was bottled up inside his bulk. He decided to listen to an album and then ring a few birds to see if any of them wanted to come round. Terry hung up his flight jacket and put the kettle on before flicking through his records. He lingered over 'Oi! Oi! Music' by The Oppressed, then considered putting on Combat 84. In the end he pulled out a Close Shave long-player and slapped it on to his deck.

Terry made himself a pot of peppermint tea as the Birmingham skinheads stormed through their anthem 'Oi Kinnock Give Us Back Our Rose'. This thoroughgoing denunciation of the Labour Party brought a smile to Blake's lips. How anyone could seriously invoke the name of St George against what they took to be anti-patriotic Parliamentarians was beyond Terry. When you added to this some spectacularly inept lead guitar licks, the progeny was a classic of far-Right reaction.

Next up was 'Scrounger' and then 'Telly Addict'. Terry sipped at his herb tea as Close Shave launched into one of his all-time Oi! favourites. 'Sunday Sport' was the ultimate in street rock, a song so crass it made Sham seem sophisticated. Fluffy had to be the most lumpen of proletarians to shout out his desire to bed pin-up girls. This was the authentic sound of working-class Britain and Terry loved it! It combined a great riff with lyrics so dumb they could only have been written by a genius. Guaranteed to get up the noses of arty-farty trendies, it provided conclusive proof that class was as much a cultural as a political and an economic construct. Blake's thoughts on this matter were interrupted by someone banging on the door.

'Hello.' It was the bird he'd chatted up in the lift. 'Got any dance music?'

'Is Model 500 OK?' Terry asked as he ushered her in and took the Close Shave album off his deck.

'It's really old,' she said as he put on 'Electronic', 'but it'll do.'

The blonde wrapped her arms around Blake's neck and proceeded to thrust her crutch against him. Their lips met and the girl forced her tongue into the skinhead's mouth. Using her forearms, she applied considerable pressure to his shoulders. Terry found himself on his knees. He lifted up the blonde's leather miniskirt and quickly ascertained that she wasn't wearing any knickers. The girl was so wet that if she'd stood on her hands Blake could have taken a swim in her twat. The blonde pressed the boot-boy's head against her cunt. Taking the hint, he began to lick her out.

Five

Rupert Dawson-Rand had walked the length of Turner Street without finding the building. It was not a long road but it contained so many offices and clinics connected to the London Hospital that he was by no means the first person to have difficulty locating the unnumbered door he required. Rupert scratched his balls, he was desperate for a piss. He walked back to Commercial Road and then turned round. This was all he needed! On top of the fact that some skinhead had been undermining his authority by talking nonsense to the membership of My One Flesh, he couldn't find the fucking clinic! He decided to abort the mission and head over to the Whitechapel Gallery where he could relieve himself and perfect his pick-up technique on some arty tart. If he had no joy with the latter, he'd simply go on to Freedom and purchase stock for his stall.

As he neared the northern end of the street, the words SPECIAL CLINIC caught Rupert's attention. He stepped through a pedestrian access point situated to the left of a wrought-iron gate and found himself standing on a hospital driveway. He advanced a few paces, took in a sign directing women patients to a basement level entrance, looked back and saw his view of the directions into the male section had been obscured by builders' scaffolding. Rupert was relieved to find a toilet located in the entrance to the clinic.

'Excuse me,' a nurse shouted after him as he walked into the bog.

'Yes?' Rupert muttered as he turned round in the doorway.

'Please act upon that request,' the brunette said, pointing to a sign which read PATIENTS ARE ASKED NOT TO PASS WATER BEFORE BEING EXAMINED.

The nurse then walked through a door and into another room. Rupert found a dozen hostile stares had been turned upon him. Since he wished to be taken as a genuine patient, the pro-situ accepted that for the time being he would not be able to take a leak. Swallowing hard, he shuffled over to the reception desk.

'Been here before?' another woman demanded.

'No.'

'Fill in this form.'

Rupert had trouble getting his eyes to focus on the questions as he desperately fought the rising pain in his bladder. He gave a false name and address but was honest enough to admit that he'd come of his own volition rather than being referred by his doctor. He handed the form back to the receptionist who glanced over it before assigning him a number and writing this on to a card. 'Bring this every time you come for treatment,' she said, handing him the chit. 'When it's your turn to be examined, the doctor will call out your name.'

'How long will that be?' the pro-situ asked.

'Judging by the queue in front of you, I'd say about fifteen minutes.'

'I'm desperate for a piss. Do you think I could be examined immediately,' he pleaded.

'I'm afraid that's not possible,' the receptionist hissed and then added, after smiling sarcastically, 'You'll just have to wait your turn.'

Rupert paced the room, barely taking in its other occupants. Most of those waiting to be seen were young – in their late teens or early twenties. There was an overweight bloke of Rupert's age slouched in a corner reading a copy of *Penthouse*. The youngsters horsed about and made a lot of noise. The only patient to conduct himself with any dignity was fiftyish, impeccably dressed and had a back as straight as a ramrod.

'Oi, darling, give us yer phone number,' one of the teenagers shouted at a passing nurse.

'Don't talk to Nick, he's got clap!' screamed another.

'You fucking slag, what's the matter with you? I've got dosh if there's a meter on your cunt. I could show you a good time, bitch!' the first youth shouted after the sister as she walked through a door.

'Mind your language,' the impeccably dressed man snapped at the teenager.

'Fuck off back to Africa!' Nick screamed.

'Yeah, ethnic,' his friend continued. 'I'm in the NF – whatcha gonna do about it?'

'You've got no respect for anybody,' the man said coldly. 'I refuse to lower myself to your level.'

'You fuckin' tosser!'

Rupert knew he ought to intervene on the man's behalf but somehow he couldn't bring himself to do so. He rationalized his inaction on the grounds that if he got into a fight he was likely to wet himself. The argument fizzled out and very soon afterwards the pro-situ was called up. A doctor asked him a series of questions. After Rand lied about experiencing a pain when he passed water and having fucked twenty different women in the past month, he was sent off for tests.

'I'm bursting for a piss,' Rupert said, interrupting the technician who was explaining the examination procedure. 'Can't I give you a urine sample now?'

'This is highly irregular,' he was told.

'I'm going to wet myself,' the pro-situ sobbed.

The technician gave Rand a sterilized container and pointed him in the direction of a cubicle fitted out with a wash-basin and toilet. Rupert was barely able to contain himself as he fished his cock from his flies. Seconds later, a veritable torrent of piss had filled the jar and the discharge was flowing over the rim, down Rand's hand and splashing across the floor.

The pro-situ used toilet-paper to wipe up the worst of the mess. He left the urine at a collection-point and returned to the cubicle in which the technician would complete his examination. The bit he liked best was when the orderly took his prick in a rubber-gloved hand and stuck a needle inside to take a sample of the internal tissue. Rupert had been to clap clinics all over London and the Home Counties but he'd yet to be examined by a woman. Until that glorious day came, he'd continue consoling himself with boasts of his sexual conquests and honest enough accounts of his regular check-ups.

The doctor instructed him to come back in two weeks' time to be told the results of his test. Rand went up to the reception desk and attempted to make an appointment.

'I'm afraid you'll just have to come and queue up,' he was told. 'We don't have an appointment system.'

'Well, what about going out for a drink this Saturday?' he asked the receptionist.

'What – and catch clap! You're joking!'

'It was only a suggestion,' Rand mumbled as he slunk away.

Rupert felt more at ease once he was inside the Whitechapel Gallery. He'd had his sexual and other kicks from slumming it with the proles at the clap clinic. Going into the exhibition he felt like a prodigal son who'd returned home with a heightened appreciation for the comforts of his upper-class life-style. His family were well known as patrons of the arts and certain members had made more than merely financial contributions to the nation's heritage. Taking his cue from Debord, Rand knew that Dada and surrealism had marked the end of art. As a consequence, it had become Rupert's personal mission to realize and suppress world culture in its entirety. Art (poetry in the situationist sense) was to be abolished so that it could reappear everywhere! Rand's family disapproved of his politics simply because they'd failed to grasp that a desire to abolish the working class lay at the heart of the situationist project. After the revolution everyone would be middle class and the traditions which the European bourgeoisie had bequeathed to the world would at last become a truly universal culture.

'A particularly bold use of line,' Rupert said to a girl who was making a close study of a blue canvas with a yellow stripe running down one edge.

'And the colour!' she cried. 'It brings tears to my eyes!'

'I can see your senses are tuned to the finer things in life, indeed to spiritual values,' Rand said grandly, 'and so I'm sure you'll accept my request for your company when I dine at Boswell's tomorrow night.'

'I'm afraid my husband is taking me to the opera,' the young woman replied.

'But the dining-room is Edwardian,' Rand protested, 'and freshly cut flowers are laid out on each table!'

'I'm only recently married and I'm not in the habit of taking meals in romantic settings with men who frequent East End art establishments.'

'You don't understand!' the pro-situ rasped in exasperation. 'The menu consists chiefly of game and pastries, the house wine is probably the best you'll ever taste in the class!'

'Please leave me in peace.'

'Trollop,' Rupert screamed. 'I'll not listen to any more of your perverted suggestions. How dare you assail my ears with such filth. I won't besmirch myself by speaking to a harlot who wants me to ram my big, hard cock up her hot, creamy slit!'

The disturbance caught the attention of a museum guard who ushered the woman out of the gallery. There was much tut-tutting from other visitors and after a few minutes a member of the management appeared, to apologize to Rupert about the incident. 'Unfortunately,' he explained, 'with our policy of bringing culture to the working classes, we get the occasional bad egg visiting the gallery. As I'm sure you appreciate, these savages need to be exposed to an incredible amount of art before its civilizing influence really becomes operational. Indeed, the majority of the brutes who live in the local area are intellectually stunted and so there's very little we can do for them.'

Rupert assured the curator that the indignity he'd suffered would not cloud his view of the work being done at the Whitechapel. Rand then wandered off to the gallery bookshop, where he took a professional interest in the stock. There was a great deal he could buy here to resell to the leftie wankers who patronized his stall in Camden Market. Rand selected monographs on Gilbert and George, Max Ernst, Malevich, Tatlin, Andy Warhol and Joseph Beuys. These were expensive hardbacks with lots of colour reproductions. The pro-situ was looking forward to realizing and suppressing their value by battering the books with a hammer and thereby fooling his customers into believing they were second-hand. As he paid for the merchandise with a credit card, he couldn't help but feel smug about the ruse he'd adopted to account for the wealth he flaunted in the course of his political activities. He'd become an international legend after telling every anarchist who'd listen that his money came from stealing new books, battering fuck out of them and then selling the damaged goods to bargain hunters.

Rand locked himself into a cubicle in the men's toilet. He removed the books from their carrier and placed them in another bag. He shredded the bag he'd been given in the gallery shop and flushed it down the loo. Then the pro-situ let himself out of the toilet and strode over to Freedom.

'Get yer hair cut, 'ave a barf!' two museum guards who happened to be relieving themselves shouted after Rand as he left.

'Fuckin' typical,' one of them said. 'These upper-class wankers think they're so superior with their bullshit culture and yet most of them don't even wash their hands after taking a crap.'

'You have to be a degenerate to like modern art,' the other observed knowledgeably.

'Yeah,' his mate replied, 'everyone knows the ruling class is decadent and that their culture simply reflects the fact that they're subhuman.'

'That's why decent people stay out of this place – the only workers you ever see in 'ere are us and the cleaners.'

'I'd never 'ave taken the job if I 'adn't been desperate for work.'

'Me too.'

Rupert could smell the ink from the Aldgate Press print-shop as he climbed the stairs to Freedom. Having reached his destination, the pro-situ was surprised to clock a face which had disappeared from the anarchist scene several years before. He couldn't put a name to the features but decided he might as well be friendly.

'Alright?' Rand inquired.

'Yeah,' came the reply. 'And you?'

'Great,' Rupert said, opening his bag so that the monographs could be seen. 'Look what I just nicked from the art gallery next door.'

'What you gonna do with the books?'

'Sell them, of course. I've got a second-hand stall in Camden Market.'

'I know the rest of My One Flesh, they're mates of mine. I bet they're jealous of your American Express card.'

'Who are you? What are you talking about?'

'I'm Terry Blake and I just happened to be walking past the gallery bookshop as you were at the cash till.'

'I just bought a couple of postcards as a decoy,' the pro-situ lied.

'No you didn't, I saw you pay for those books!'

'You don't have to shout,' Rand complained. 'I'm not deaf.'

'I'm not dumb,' Terry grinned. 'If you wanna keep our conversation private, why don't you buy me a coffee somewhere comrades are unlikely to overhear us talking?'

'What about the café in the Whitechapel Gallery,' Rand suggested.

'You'll have to buy me a pastry as well,' Blake snarled. 'I'll need something to keep me sweet in such a disgusting atmosphere.'

'I've got a credit card, you know,' Rupert whined as he followed Terry down the stairs.

The trendies visiting the Whitechapel made Blake want to puke but they didn't make him as sick as scum like Rand. At least the artsy-fartsy crowd didn't harbour a missionary zeal to convert the so-called *lower classes* and *lower races* to their white, bourgeois, patriarchal culture. These wankers were simply snobs, and the way in which they oppressed ordinary people was relatively straightforward and easy enough to combat. The pro-situ was a different kettle of fish. While pretending to oppose bourgeois culture, he actually represented its avant-garde. His background of money and public-school privilege gave him the confidence to turn up at anarchist meetings where he'd attempt to pass himself off as a proletarian while simultaneously imposing an alien culture on any worker who happened to be present. Central to Rand's programme were bourgeois notions of aesthetic distancing which had been transposed from the cultural to the political plane. Among these was the situationist concept of the Spectacle, the idea that everything that was directly lived has moved away into representation. What Rand wanted to do was remake the human community in the image of bourgeois ideology.

Terry had known various ex-public-school boys in the anarchist movement. They tended to claim all systems of education were equally oppressive. He would never accept this. While the privileged few in their boarding-schools were told, year in and year out, that as adults they'd rule the world – the children of workers were drilled to believe they were worthless. Blake had gone to school on a GLC overspill estate where day after day it had been drummed into his mind that he was shit.

Terry looked around the Whitechapel and was disgusted. At school he'd been told he was too stupid to participate in the high culture of which the paintings on display represented a small part. Of course the teachers ignored the fact that Blake and his mates had no desire to waste their time on this garbage. Coming as he did from a lower-middle-class background, Terry had opportunities denied to most of his school-friends. He'd had the option of being like his parents and aping the manners of the upper middle class – and of being sneered at behind his back for lacking the truly refined tastes that come from years of inbreeding and a thoroughly poisoned gene pool. Blake chose the other alternative – working-class culture in the form of punk rock and skinheadism.

Terry sat down at a table in the gallery café while Rand fetched him coffee and a Danish. He eyed up the birds and knew that it was his refusal to ape middle-class manners that enabled him to have any woman he wanted. He did not accept his station in life and would not stick to it. He smiled when he remembered the graffiti campaigns he'd organized at school before sports and governors' days – swastikas and slogans supporting the IRA and PLO. He'd always succeeded in offending the teachers and their guests. Then there was the time he'd initiated the slow handclap at a prize-giving attended by outside dignitaries. Afterwards, his year was told they'd disgraced themselves. Although he'd never bothered to read them, he'd made a point of walking around school with books by Mao and Marx and paid a price for that. The senior master had stopped him every day for three years when he was coming in from the playground – to check he was using the door assigned to members of his house. Another time he'd been caned for failing to remember that, when he was addressing a member of staff, each sentence had to be completed with the word 'sir'. Despite the victimization, the bastards had failed to break Terry's spirit. He'd learnt early the most effective ways of directing his hatred against those in authority and was rightly proud of the king-sized chip on his shoulder.

'Is . . . is . . . is an apricot filling suitable?' Rand stammered as he placed two coffees and a pastry on the table.

'It's fine,' Blake informed him.

'Good, I hope our differences can be sorted out as easily,' Rupert said with a bit more confidence.

'There aren't any differences,' Terry spat. 'All I'm interested in is revolution and the start of the next evolutionary phase. I just want to make it clear that you should avoid getting in the way of what I'm doing.'

'I wouldn't dream of interfering,' Rand assured him.

'Good, then you'll encourage the membership of My One Flesh to remortgage their house to raise the dosh for a nuclear warhead.'

'But the idea's ludicrous,' the pro-situ protested.

'No it's not,' Blake rebuked him. 'I know where I can get the warhead. I just need a hundred thousand pounds to pay for it.'

'But the Nicolson brothers will never agree to mortgaging their house. They sunk the money they inherited from their paternal grandmother into it.'

'They'd better decide to raise the cash one way or another,' Terry snapped malevolently, 'or else I'm gonna have to let them know you've never stolen a book in your life. And if that happens, you'll not only cease to lead your little group, you'll become the laughing-stock of the milieu.'

'Are you suggesting I'm to persuade them to mortgage their house?'

'Yes.'

'I can't do it.'

'Think about your reputation, about never being able to show your face on the anarchist scene again.'

'Will you let me know when and where you're going to detonate the bomb so that I can make sure I'm well away from the blast?'

'Sure.'

'Let's shake on it,' Rand said, sticking out his hand.

'Let's just say it's a deal,' Terry replied coldly. 'Personally, I don't go in for Masonic rituals like hand-shaking.'

'You sound like a right-wing conspiracy theorist.'

'At least I'm not a King's Road flake,' Blake snarled.

'That's unfair,' the pro-situ whimpered. 'I can't help where I was born.'

'No one can,' Terry replied, 'but you're still responsible for what you are. Unlike you, I've never tried to make out I was born a prole. I despise the lower middle class but I've never denied that's my social origins. You're a fuckin' hypocrite refusing to admit you was born rich.'

'But all my family's wealth is in property, they don't own the means of production. Objectively speaking I don't come from a bourgeois background.'

'Shut up!' Blake snapped. 'I don't wanna listen to your bullshit. Go and tell the Nicolson brothers that they're to fill a suitcase with a hundred thousand in small denomination notes. I'll collect it from them tomorrow night.'

Rand got up from his seat and left. Terry bit off a corner of his pastry and took another sip of coffee. While appraising the talent, he decided he fancied a bit of posh. He caught the eye of a redhead carrying a tray of food. She walked over to where Blake was sitting and placed her dinner on the table.

'Do you mind if I join you?'

'Be my guest, red,' Terry replied, betraying the fact that he'd read one too many Mickey Spillane novels.

'I'm Sarah. I don't like Americanisms.'

'I'm Terry – you can call me Tel.'

'What did you make of the exhibition, Terence?' Sarah asked as she tucked into an overpriced salad.

'Nothing. I don't like art, I just came in here to strike a deal.'

'You're not making much of an effort to be friendly.'

'I don't have to. You love it, doll.'

'And what would you say if I moved to another table?'

'That you're frigid.'

'You've got a very high opinion of yourself.'

'I take it you've got a car.'

'Yes.'

'And a free afternoon.'

'Yes.'

'And you're gonna drive us back to my place.'

'Yes.'

'I rest my case.'

Terry leant back in his chair and relaxed. He'd no illusions about what this bird wanted. She saw him as a bit of rough, a pet with whom she could indulge her masochistic feelings. And if that was what this upper-class bitch wanted, Blake was more than willing to treat her like shit. As long as he kept playing dumb, his brand of genetic ecstasy would throw her right out of orbit.

'What do you do?' Sarah asked.

'I make porno videos.'

'You look like you work on a building site.'

'I prefer sitting on my arse.' Terry grinned as he said it. 'I'm also working on a book about incredibly strange sexploitation movies.'

'That doesn't exactly make you an intellectual,' Sarah said, somewhat annoyed by the obvious relish with which the skinhead had spilled the beans about his sick trade.

'It makes me a living,' Terry shot back.

'I hope you've got a thirteen-inch cock,' the redhead sneered.

'Flaccid or erect?' Blake demanded.

70

'Come on, let's go,' the rich girl said as she got up from the table. 'I want to see just how big your prick is.'

Terry directed her through Mile End, then Limehouse and on to the West India Dock Road. When Sarah parked her MG outside the flats, Blake warned her to take anything of value up to his pad. He said this because it was what she wanted to hear. He'd met enough of her kind to understand she was a bored bourgeoise who craved excitement and danger.

'Paki, Paki!' two three-year-olds chanted at a pensioner who was walking down the street. The old man didn't bat an eyelid, he simply carried on as if nothing had happened. Terry was impressed with the way in which he maintained his pride and dignity despite this onslaught of racial abuse. You couldn't blame the kids, they were too young to understand what they were doing. They simply copied the behaviour of older whites who were eaten up with race hatred. The incident brought home to Blake the terrible sickness of wankers involved in operations such as *Anti-Fascist Probe*. They equated racism with fascism for political gain. While fascists were undoubtedly responsible for a number of vicious racial attacks, the actual membership of these far-Right groups was minuscule. Most East End racists were also working-class socialists who wouldn't have voted National Front or British National Party in a million years. They had no time for tinpot dictators who dreamt of a new Nazi regime. While Terry insisted that fascism was racist, he sincerely believed there'd be little progress within the field of grass-roots community relations until the equation of racism and fascism was broken. Indeed it seemed that anti-fascism was a ploy on the part of those who benefited from institutionalized racism to direct attention away from their own brand of bigotry.

Sarah wrinkled her nose as she got into the lift. It smelt like a toilet. Terry pressed the button for the twenty-third floor and the doors clanked shut. Once they got into his flat, Blake began setting up his video equipment.

'Are you intending to film us having sex?' Sarah asked in amazement.

'Yeah.'

'What makes you think I'll allow you to make this video?'

'You can wear a ski-mask if you want,' Terry told her.

Sarah decided she found the prospect of becoming a porno star quite exciting. She looked through Blake's record collection and quickly ascertained that most of it consisted of skinhead bands.

'Have you got anything classical?' she asked.

'No,' Terry told her.

'What do you want me to put on?'

'Any Cock Sparrer album.'

Sarah pulled out *True Grit* and slapped the second side on to Terry's deck. The song titles seemed typical of what Blake would listen to – 'Runnin' Riot', then 'Chip on My Shoulder' and so on.

'Are you ready to fuck me?' Sarah wanted to know as she pulled off her clothes.

'Once you've blown me,' Terry replied. 'Kneel here,' he said after he'd manoeuvred her across the room.

Blake darted behind the camera and adjusted the focus. He stripped off and flicked a switch which left the camcorder running. Sarah took his cock in her hand and squeezed it. Once it had hardened she began licking the tip with her tongue. This procedure activated a genetic code buried at the very centre of Blake's brain. His kick was to fight against the Dictatorship of the D N A and today he chose to do so by reciting a passage from Richard Jefferies's autobiography.

'I was utterly alone with the sun and the earth,' Terry announced, 'lying down on the grass, I spoke to my soul, to the earth, the sun, the air, and the distant sea far beyond sight.'

Christ, thought Sarah, my piece of rough is even kinkier than I imagined. He's got bulges in all the right places and a warp in his brain.

'I thought of the earth's firmness,' Blake continued. 'I felt it bear me up; through the grassy couch there came an influence as if I could hear the great earth speaking to me.'

Terry had left the Isle of Dogs. The way Sarah was working the base of his cock with her hand and its tip with her mouth had put him back in touch with his genetic roots. As his voice droned on, it took on the quality of a recording that was being played back through millions of years of sexual history.

'I spoke to the sea; though so far, in my mind I saw it, green at the rim of the earth and blue in the deeper ocean.'

Blake was oblivious to the fact that the redhead had pushed him on to his back and was guiding his throbbing member into her black hole of a cunt.

'I desired to have its strength, its mystery and glory.'

72

Sarah was working herself up and down Terry's fuck stick, beating out the one rhythm guaranteed to draw forth more of the skinhead's ancient speech.

'I turned to the blue heaven over, going into its depth, inhaling its exquisite colour and sweetness.'

The redhead was beginning to believe that her pick-up was an android. His trance presented her with a challenge. She was determined to end this prerecorded speech and draw forth his genetic inheritance.

'By all these I prayed, I felt an emotion of the soul beyond all definition; prayer is a puny thing to it.'

'I want to feel your balls banging against me!' Sarah squealed as she broke her rhythm and rolled over so that Blake ended up on top of her. 'Fuck me, for Christ's sake fuck me. I wanna feel your spunk spurting inside me.'

The words cut through Terry's brain, and although he didn't consciously process their meaning, he nevertheless acted upon their content. His horny bit of posh screamed in ecstasy as she felt the skinhead's balls bang against her flesh.

'By the blue heaven, by the rolling sun bursting through untrodden space, a new ether every day unveiled.'

Without knowing it, Terry was pumping, pumping up the volume towards orgasm. Sarah was bellowing obscenities, raking her finger-nails up and down Blake's back and in the process drawing blood.

'Then . . . then . . .' Terry stammered, 'then returning I. . . .' Molten genetics spurted through his prick and a fire burned in his brain.

'You're a fucking animal!' Sarah hissed as she experienced orgasm as a genetic replay of her family's centuries' old tradition of sexually abusing their serfs and servants.

The two of them lay panting on the floor for several minutes, then Sarah pushed Terry from her chest. She got up and dressed. The camcorder filmed the skinhead lying in a state of exhaustion as the rich bitch left his flat. The redhead was conscious of Blake's come dribbling from her cunt as she waited for the lift to take her down to her car. It was testimony to the best fuck she'd ever had.

Six

'What's wrong with the bastards?' Inspector Stephens roared. 'Are they yellow cowards afraid to face the full might of the British state when it sets out to crush them?'

'Maybe Arthur will have some ideas about how we should proceed,' Brian Smith suggested helpfully.

'That wanker should've been here ten minutes ago! Since Roberts and his mates at Seven sold me this bill of goods, they'd better 'ave a plausible explanation as to why the blacks aren't riotin'. I've stuck my neck out forcin' through this operation and I'm expecting a pay-off.'

'What about me?' Smith complained. 'Roberts 'as wrecked my political career by makin' me claim it was ethnics what done me over!'

'Stop whining, you fuckin' scum-sucker!' Stephens snapped. 'You threw everythin' away after the '79 election. You've got nothin' to lose. I have a professional position and the lefties who've got the council stitched up are baying for my blood. If this don't come off right, I could find myself in very hot water indeed!'

'You're just fuckin' selfish!' Smith bleated. 'You've no conception of the spiritual dimensions to our struggle for racial survival.'

'Bickering again, boys?' Arthur Roberts remarked as he walked into the room.

'You're fifteen minutes late,' the inspector complained, 'and who's this bird you've got with you?'

'This is Joyce Grant. She's a colleague of mine from Seven. Joyce, this is Inspector James Stephens.'

Joyce shook hands with the copper and then went through the same ritual with Brian Smith. After eyeing the hippy up, both the inspector and the Third Positionist concluded that they'd like to give this degenerate little slut a good knobbing.

'Joyce', Roberts explained, 'is working undercover. She's infiltrated the Sandringham Road drugs scene and will now brief you on the current mood among the pushers. According

74

to her information, we miscalculated the likely reaction to last night's raid.'

'You see, gentlemen,' Grant said, coming in on cue, 'the last thing the Sandringham Road soul brothers want is trouble. Outbreaks of lawlessness disrupt their business activities. Most of the whites who buy pot from them are middle-class wimps who'd run a mile rather than risk their lives in a dangerous part of town. The brothers have a policy of cracking down on muggers and other antisocial elements. This sound and sensible approach to their trade means that, despite a justified hatred of racist cops, as far as possible they avoid ruckin' the police.'

'You make these ethnics sound like responsible people when they're actually plying a trade of death,' the inspector complained. 'And besides, what's wrong with being racist?'

'Jim,' Roberts put in, 'at Seven we take a long-term view of things. We've no evidence to suggest that anything stronger than Class B drugs is being sold in Sandringham Road. Joyce is regularly exposed to horrors which make pot-peddlers look like nursery-school children. She's currently investigating a guy called Terry Blake who's a very nasty piece of work indeed. He produces vile anarchist pornography. The videos he's putting out would make your stomach churn. We also have reason to believe he's using the profits from this foul trade to subvert the British state.'

'Forget what I said,' Stephens said magnanimously. 'Let's set to work. We need a plan which will get these immigrants rioting.'

The inspector's gutter racism reaffirmed Grant's recently lowered opinion of the police and intelligence services. She'd been recruited into Seven by Roberts, who'd used his Leninist credentials to convince her that the organization was kosher. During her probationary period, Joyce had been surprised to discover that a vast number of leftists were members of the intelligence community. Seven's existence remained a closely guarded secret and this had enabled its agents to escape the mole-hunting that had caused such damage to the efficiency of Five and Six. Beyond those in the security services and a few uniformed police officers, only the Prime Minister was briefed on the activities of this élite security squad. To date, Seven had avoided the scrutiny of those MPs who crusaded for votes by demanding that the ranks of British spydom be purged of Reds. While portraits of Marx, Lenin and other radical heroes lined

75

the corridors of the squad's headquarters in St John's Wood, the organization was thoroughly opposed to anarchism and all other forms of anti-parliamentary deviation. It was this fanatical devotion to the concept of democracy that placed Seven at the centre of Britain's counter-subversion strategy. Recently, the key role played by so-called communists in maintaining the British state had led Joyce to question the credibility of Leninism as a revolutionary creed.

'The country would be up shit creek if it wasn't for Seven,' Roberts spat. 'We're the brains who devise the solutions when our uniformed counterparts find themselves out of their depth.'

'Yes, sir!' Joyce affirmed.

'Now you see, Jim,' Roberts continued, 'we need to raise the stakes. We have to do something that'll really anger the soul brothers. That means coming up with something better than busting a few of the bastards for peddling dope.'

'And what exactly does this entail?' the copper demanded.

'Give Joyce a list of those you arrested,' Roberts instructed.

The inspector took a sheet of paper from a desk drawer and passed it to the hippy.

'Look down the list, Joyce,' the spymaster hissed, 'and cross out the names of all those who are actually pushing drugs.'

'None of these people deal in Sandringham Road,' Joyce sighed as she ran her eyes over the names.

'Don't worry 'bout it,' Stephens put in, 'we planted dope on all of 'em.'

'Very good, inspector,' Roberts snapped sarcastically. 'OK, Joyce, give the list to Smith.'

As she did so, her boss told the Third Positionist to pick a name. Smith couldn't work out what the hell was going on and so presumed that he'd been entrusted with a very important task. He spent a long time studying the document that had been passed to him.

'Freddie Love,' the fascist said at last.

'What we're gonna do', Roberts informed his captive audience, 'is kill the guy Brian picked. A death in custody always gets the soul brothers hoppin' mad. Jim, do you fancy taking care of the execution?'

'No way,' the copper shot back.

'Well, Brian,' the anti-fascist purred malevolently, 'it looks like you've finally got a chance to strike a blow for your race.'

'I won't do it!' Smith screeched. 'You've already forced me into compromising my political position. If I did this, it'd be hangin' over my head and you'd be forever threatening me with further investigations into Freddie Love's death.'

'Very well, I'll do it myself.'

'I thought you were an anti-fascist!' Joyce thundered.

'I've dedicated my life to the anti-racist cause, slut!' her boss snapped. 'And watch out, 'coz you're in breach of discipline. To avoid further insubordination I'll explain the necessity of my actions. Sometimes sacrifices have to be made for the movement. I've spent most of my adult life fighting racism and fascism. When I launched *Anti-Fascist Probe* it was not as a front for the security services, I did so out of a modest private income. It was at this time that I began to collaborate with Seven. A few years later I actually joined our noble service which, as you know, is made up of whites who believe that the rights of all people should be defended by a communist alliance operating from within the British state. The time has come for blacks to make a few trifling sacrifices. These will enable us to pursue their cause with renewed vigour. I'll explain all this to Freddie before I immortalize him. I'm sure I can make Love understand that I'm simply assigning him a small but vital role in the war for progress.'

'Yes, sir,' Grant replied flatly, finally convinced that her boss was actually mad. She was glad she'd warned assorted dope-dealers about impending raids. They'd come to realize that what she said was not to be taken lightly. She had to reach these soul brothers at the earliest possible moment and warn them about this latest threat to their liberty. The writing was on the wall for the so-called anti-fascist movement because this time Roberts was going too far. As always, black youth would quickly adapt to the new situation and learn to organize against the wankers from the *Probe*. Quite rightly, they weren't prepared to wait for bastards like Roberts to smash the system that discriminated against them. Their people's struggle had a long history, and when this noble cause triumphed it would be as a result of their own efforts and not via a series of piecemeal concessions won for them by a handful of white reformers who were eaten up by *inverted* racism and liberal guilt.

'Right,' Roberts said, returning to the business in hand, 'if I shoot Love tomorrow lunch-time, then we can have the blacks rioting before it gets dark. Brian, I want your men to wade in against them.'

'You're forgetting that I now run a Third Positionist outfit,' the fascist replied. 'My membership isn't made up of hard-core white supremacists and, given our ideological orientation, I can't just order them to fight blacks.'

'Listen, sunshine,' the anti-fascist snapped, 'I fund your paper and I also read the damn thing. I know for a fact that you've called for the death penalty to be used against those who deal drugs. I'm not asking your membership to take on Rasta Nation, they're simply doing over a bunch of pushers who happen to be black.'

'Oh, alright,' Smith conceded.

'I'll send you some of my men to make up your numbers,' Roberts said. 'Your membership is too small to cause serious trouble without additional help.'

'Are you talking 'bout agents from the service?' the Third Positionist demanded.

'You're not meant to know about Seven.'

'All I wanna know is whether or not these men are from the security service!' Smith shouted.

'I can't send my agents to help you out,' Roberts hissed. 'You'll simply get cannon-fodder from the anti-fascist movement.'

'My men insist on the highest level of ideological coherence,' the fascist replied indignantly. 'They'll never agree to fight alongside elements from a Leninist organization.'

'I've financed your Brownshirt movement from day one, so your men better be out on the street tomorrow night!' the anti-fascist howled as he slammed his fist against the inspector's desk.

'Cockney Nation is fighting a war of national liberation,' Smith pontificated. 'It is an independent force which will not allow itself to be compromised by Leninists.'

'I'll brief a squad of white anti-fascists to pass themselves off as Nazis,' Roberts hissed. 'If your cadre won't fight alongside these men, they'll have to help out the blacks. Should your troops fail to participate in this ruck, I'll axe the funding of your paper.'

'We are a Third Force,' the fascist said grandly, 'who will fight to win. For the time being, it suits us to struggle alongside those we will later repatriate to their ancestral homelands. Once the overlords of Westminster have been expelled from our country, no one will impose black immigration upon us.'

'You can't be serious!' Joyce exclaimed.

'Do you think I'd devote my life to the Third Position if I wasn't fully convinced of the justice of the Cockney cause?' Smith spat.

'Either you're mad or I'm having my leg pulled,' the hippy jeered.

'He's insane,' Roberts snapped, 'and this is one of the many reasons I've devoted my life to anti-fascist activity. But we've talked enough, Joyce. Now you've provided us with the information we required, you're dismissed.'

Worry-lines creased Grant's forehead as she left the police station. The hippy no longer wanted anything to do with Arthur Roberts and his sick manipulation of the anti-fascist movement. She wondered whether her psychopathic boss would ever allow her to walk away from his organization.

'Hey, Joy, you look like you're carrying the weight of the world on your shoulders.'

Joyce turned her head and saw Winston Ingliss walking towards her. She'd drifted to Sandringham Road without even realizing it. Ingliss traded sinsemilla and had been Joyce's lover until the day his wife caught them screwing on the marital bed. Since that fateful afternoon more than a year ago, she'd often spoken to Winston in the street but he'd always refused her entreaties to bonk in back alleys and other similarly seedy locations. Grant knew her former lover enjoyed the respect of all the other dealers in the Hackney area and was therefore just the man to put the anti-rioting message across.

'Christ, I'm glad to see you,' she said as she put her arms around Winston and hugged him.

'Cheer up, doll. Things can't be that bad.'

Ingliss was grim-faced by the time Joyce finished her story. He understood from bitter experience the necessity of organizing against racists and political manipulators. Usually this meant getting a posse of soul brothers and their white mates together to show that they would not tolerate attempts at intimidation. Persuading the Sandringham Road mob not to retaliate against murderous provocation would be impossible. And knowing as he did that Freddie Love had been sentenced to death by a so-called anti-fascist, Ingliss could not simply stand by and allow this to happen. He was already laying plans to organize a raiding party which would free all the comrades from the police cells. Without prisoners, that bastard Roberts wouldn't have anyone to kill.

'You leave this to me, Joy,' Winston said reassuringly. 'I'll sort everything out.'

Joyce watched from afar as Ingliss engaged his mates in what became a heated conversation. She smiled as she remembered how much she'd loved running her hands over his muscular body. When it eventually dawned on her to check the time, she was thrown into a panic. Terry struck her as the impatient type. He wasn't likely to hang around Camden tube station if she was late. Grant blew a kiss in Winston's direction and then ran to catch a North London Link train from Hackney Central.

Terry checked the time and tried to ignore the sound of the baby screaming. It was early and he just wanted to get back to sleep. Janet Hobbes turned over and put her arms around Blake. She did not believe in spoiling the ten-month-old offspring of her failed marriage. Orphaned at the age of three, Janet had quickly learnt to stand on her own two feet. She hated her child for his helplessness. Ronald would remain a burden until he'd grown up enough to run errands for her. She put up with his bratish behaviour because as her only son he'd be obliged to look after his mum as soon as he began earning regular wages. As far as Janet could see, blood-ties were the only ones that really counted. The marriage to Tom had been a miscalculation on her part. She'd figured on him providing her with a decent standard of living but, within weeks of hitching the knot, he'd taken to blowing all his earnings down the boozer. He'd even had the cheek to claim this was a means of escaping her incessant nagging!

Janet placed her hand on Terry's love muscle and massaged his growing erection. She pressed her lips against his mouth while simultaneously trying to total up the number of her friends this stallion had taken. It was impossible to calculate – every woman on the estate seemed to have had his balls out at some point over the previous five years. After moving

80

into his twenty-third-storey flat in Cockroach City, Blake had quickly gained a reputation both for his sexual skills and the willingness with which he'd demonstrate them to any passable bird.

The single mother guided Terry into the site of her mystery. These two rebels enjoyed an early morning fuck while ten-month-old Ronald screamed in the background. Janet wasn't aware that her child was crying. She'd left the Isle of Dogs and was basking in the Californian sun after being discovered by a top Hollywood producer. For Terry, sexual ecstasy was the equivalent of single-handedly wiping out the entire population of Britain. As he came, he imagined his orgasm to be an all-out nuclear attack on what brain-dead patriots insisted was his country.

'Oh God,' the girl moaned, 'you make me feel so good when you come inside me. When you're pumping your love juice into my cunt it seems like Terry 'n' Janet are the only things which are real. Come on, big boy, fuck me some more!'

The skinhead obliged. He could keep himself hard through sheer force of will. While other men went flaccid after shooting their load, Blake was a law unto himself. Terry'd always liked talkers, screamers, birds who felt compelled to tell him he was the best thing since sliced bread. He'd honed his sexual skills to the point where he could make even the silent types beg him to screw their brains out. With Janet it was easy, Blake hardly made any effort at all.

'Fuck me, baby, fuck me,' she moaned. 'I love it when you thrust your big cock inside me. I'd crawl through a tank full of sewage if that was what it took to make you shag me. I'd slash my wrists and beg you to give me one last fuck if you ever said you wouldn't screw me. You can have me any way you want, just as long as you're prepared to give my cunt a good thrashing.'

Terry kept up the pressure. He gradually increased the speed with which he moved in and out of Janet's love hole. Then he stopped abruptly, withdrew and grabbed a tube of KY. 'Turn over!' he barked.

Janet obeyed and her lover rubbed KY into her arse and then over his cock. Terry threw the tube of lubricant to the floor and positioned himself above the girl.

'That's my cunt,' Janet squealed as the skinhead re-entered her.

'I know it's your fuckin' cunt,' Blake replied gruffly as he pumped up the volume.

'I thought you were gonna fuck me up the arse.'

'Don't be so greedy for it. I'll get there in time but I want you to feel nice and relaxed before I start to push your shit uphill.'

The skinhead was as good as his word. He kept thrusting his prick deeper and deeper into the girl's moist love hole until she was begging him to come inside her. Terry then reduced the speed with which he was moving in and out of her twat. Janet began wriggling frantically.

'Please, please,' she was whining.

'Beg, bitch, beg!' Blake hissed as he withdrew from the girl's cunt and forced his cock against her rim of dark pleasures.

'Marx, Christ and Satan!' Janet bellowed as Terry's prick bore into her. Then she coughed phlegm and it landed in a thick blob on the pillow.

The girl's arse was tight. No other man had known this part of her body. Terry doubted his ability to hold in his love juice and decided just to go with the flow. When he came it was like the crowd at Upton Park surging forward after the Hammers scored a goal. Janet had never known such an ecstatic pleasure. The orgasm which swept through their twin bulks achieved a velocity equivalent to the speed of light.

Despite the baby's screaming both Blake and the girl fell into a sound sleep. When they woke, Terry took a quick bath and then left.

As the skinhead was walking to Crossharbour Station, a yelping dog ran at him. Blake sent his steel toe-capped DMs cracking into the creature's jaw. There was the satisfying crunch of splintering bone and the mongrel was sent flying across the street, where it landed beneath the wheels of a passing car.

'Hey you, we saw that!' two youths were shouting as they ran after Terry. He turned round to face them. The teenagers seemed surprised that he'd responded in this way and were apparently at a loss about what to do now they'd caught up with him.

'What do you want?' Blake demanded.

'We're from Cockney Nation,' one of the youths explained rather apologetically, 'and our leadership has told us that the community should police itself. A part of this responsibility consists of preventing cruelty to animals.'

'What?' Terry said, almost laughing.

'Have you never heard of Cockney Nation?' one of the youths asked indignantly.

'No,' came the reply.

'We believe that Hackney, Newham and Tower Hamlets form an ancient kingdom which must free itself from the tyranny of Westminster and Brussels. We intend to tear down the Union Jack and in its place hoist the Black Eel of Cockney Freedom. This banner will be flown at all points between Millwall, Stoke Newington, Aldgate and East Ham. We National Revolutionaries believe our country must assume its rightful place as an autonomous state within the British Family of Nations.'

'Are you supporters of Harold Denmark and the Third Position?' Terry asked.

'His mob are racist reactionaries!' one of the youths squawked. 'Cockney Nation will never allow itself to be compromised by association with a Tory imperialist!'

'But you are supporters of the Third Position?' Terry said, almost repeating himself.

'We're the only true supporters of the Third Way in this country,' the other youth pontificated.

'Then', Blake replied, 'you understand that if the human races can't live together, it's ludicrous to expect different species to get on. Animal liberation under the Third Position means the phased, humane and financially assisted repatriation of each species to a homeland of its own. While I believe in cultural and all other forms of diversity, as an upstanding Nordic I'll always defend myself when I'm attacked by a dog!'

'Christ,' the two youths replied in unison, 'we'd never thought of that!'

'Do you know about blood groups?' Terry demanded.

'No,' came the reply.

'Among Aryans, the ruling and lower classes are made up of two sets of mutually exclusive blood groups. Those with an ABO grouping are born to lead, while the rest should follow. If you can get five hundred quid together, I'll sell you a blood kit which will scientifically test the leadership abilities of your ruling council.'

'We must have this medical marvel!' the two youths chanted.

The boys gave the skinhead their names, address and phone number. As he proceeded on his way to Crossharbour Station, Terry reflected that the two fascists were worse than pro-situs. Whereas the Debordists wanted to reduce everything to a question of economics, the Third Positionists organized their entire theory around the issue of race. Neither group was capable of grasping the central role played by culture in a world which they perceived as being empty and without depth.

Terry couldn't believe his eyes when he got on the train at Crossharbour. The bird who sat down opposite him wasn't wearing any knickers. She opened her legs so that Blake got a good view of her cunt. The skinhead could feel himself salivating and swallowed hard. When the girl got off at Limehouse, she slipped Terry a piece of paper with her name and phone number written on it. Blake alighted at Tower Gateway and walked the short distance from the Light Railway terminus to Tower Hill tube. A westbound train pulled into the station as Terry reached the platform.

Gerald Fitz-Simons eyed the skinhead nervously. Gerald disliked the East End. He lived in Chelsea and had left the relative civilization of West London only because his boss at Really Radical Publishing had ordered him to do so. Simons had been to Bow, where he'd bought the European rights to the latest novel by a trendy Californian author. He did not understand why his American counterpart chose to stay with friends in a rough part of town. While Really Radical felt obliged to publish the odd novel which was nominally about working-class London, whenever Gerald marketed one of these he chose a story set in a Bohemian area such as Brixton or Notting Hill. These days even Hackney novels were acceptable to the trendies. But places like Tower Hamlets remained off the literary map because, when it came down to it, ex-public-school boys like Simons suffered from a pathological fear of the working class.

Gerald had always considered himself something of a rebel. Since his youth he'd made a point of being rude to lowly shop assistants. Sometimes he even spat at down-and-outs who were lying unconscious in the street. Simons was getting desperate for a cigarette. Ignoring the no smoking signs, he lit up. Terry had been a dedicated non-smoker all his life and hated the selfish bastards who caused such a stink with their filthy habits. When he clocked the yuppie enjoying a crafty fag in the near-empty carriage, the skin decided it was time to spring into action.

'Oi, scum-sucker!' Blake shouted as he strode towards Simons. 'Can't you fuckin' read? It says no smoking in 'ere.'

'Mind your own business,' Gerald said boldly.

'I am minding me own business,' Terry replied. 'I don't wanna choke on the smoke from your fag!'

'Well, I'm not going to stop!' Simons announced defiantly.

'I'm warnin' you,' Blake hissed, 'put out the fag before I get really mad.'

'If you ever get the chance to spit on my grave, seize it!' Gerald replied, cackling at his own witticism.

Terry wiped the smile from the bastard's face by hauling the yuppie up from his seat and hurling him against one of the automatic doors. As the upper-class twit slid to the floor, Blake sent a steel toe-capped DM cracking into his mouth. There was the satisfying crunch of splintering bone as several teeth snapped off at the root. Gerald gurgled on his own blood and then slumped unconscious. Since the train was pulling into Monument Station, Terry lifted his wallet and threw the bastard out of the carriage.

'Fuckin' drunks!' the guard swore as he watched Gerald's body tumble on to the platform.

Terry went through the wallet and removed more than two hundred quid in cash. He could never be bothered with small-time fraud so he tore up an assortment of credit cards and stuffed the pieces down the back of his seat. Then Blake went through the yuppie's brief-case. There were copies of the latest issues of Playboy and Penthouse, a London street-map, a handful of business letters and the manuscript of an unpublished novel. The latter was annotated in ·Gerald's hand. On the front he'd written: 'Johnny, this is a very witty novel about a former stockbroker who becomes a world-class fashion designer. I think we should offer to publish it if the author will change the title from *Another Seven Figure Cheque Arrived Today*, to something a bit snappier such as *I was a Millionaire Tearaway*. Give it a read and see what you think.' Terry opened the typescript and picked a passage at random:

The judge was rather taken with Simon. He liked the young man's attitude and the way he dressed. If only Britain had produced more individuals of this quality then the Empire would never have gone into such a spiral of decline. The country needed men with an ability to lead, men who were not smitten with a liberal guilt which led them to treat members of the lower orders as their equals. By sexually abusing and then ritually murdering seventeen prostitutes, Simon had shown he possessed just the qualities which would once again make Britain Great.

'There can be no doubt about the fact that you are an exceptional young man,' the judge announced as he began his summing-up. 'When you broke the law, it was simply an expression of high spirits. It would be a tragic loss to the nation if I were to imprison you as you scale the very peaks of your chosen profession. Therefore, I'm going to fine you ten pounds for each of the seventeen murders to which you have pleaded guilty. And just to show there's no question of class favouritism at work here, I'm going to add on another thirty smackers to bring the fine up to a square two hundred pounds.'

'May I pay by American Express?' Simon asked.

Cheering broke out among the cream of London's young professionals who'd packed the court throughout the trial. Simon really was such a lovable rogue!

The train pulled in at Embankment Station. Terry got off and dumped the manuscript in a litter-bin. He walked along Villiers Street and into the Strand. The rest of the morning consisted of a slow drift up the Charing Cross Road, during which he took in innumerable book shops and committed an almost equal number of thefts. By lunch-time Blake was in Oxford Street, surrounded on all sides by a throng of hard-core shoppers. These individuals had divined the mythic nature of capitalism and were frenziedly pursuing that selection of commodities on to which they'd projected their most deep-rooted desires. After this, Terry travelled the length of Tottenham Court Road. At the north end of this street he veered right and took in one of the Lawrence Corner surplus stores. Here he bought a selection of obsolete medical equipment for seven quid. This was the *blood-testing gear* he'd soon sell to the Third Positionists for five hundred pounds.

Blake ambled into the tube system at Euston. From here he hopped a train to Camden. According to his watch, he was five minutes late and yet there was no sign of Joyce. He gave her another ten minutes and then headed off to the Record and Tape Exchange. Terry wanted to pick up a few bargains before pulling a bird.

The snail's pace at which the North London Link crawled west was driving Joyce up the wall. When she finally got off at Camden Road she was more than twenty minutes late. The hippy gave herself stitch sprinting to the tube station. Since there was no sign of her man, she decided the best course of action was to check out likely looking shops. Joyce finally caught up with Terry in Rhythm Records, where he was buying an Oi! compilation. Together, they ate pizza and took in a film.

Seven

Joyce knew she'd have to confess her spy status to Terry eventually. However, the hippy didn't want to do so until after she'd left the service. It wasn't going to be easy walking away from Seven. Joyce had been privy to many of the state's most closely guarded secrets and her resignation wouldn't be accepted casually. It took some very fast talking to persuade Blake to screw her in a derelict house just around the corner from Hackney Police Station.

'If you wanna fuck outta the flat, what's wrong with a park or golf-course?' he'd complained.

'I've got this thing about empty houses,' Joyce lied.

'We can find one in Camden,' Terry shot back.

'But I've been buildin' up the vibes by goin' and wanking in this one,' Joyce persisted.

'You're really twisted, bitch,' Blake spat. 'You've mixed up hair-brained hippy beliefs with your perverted desires. It's sick, it's really sick.'

'Look, just do it to please me.'

'OK, we'll take a train from Kentish Town West.'

All the windows had been knocked out of the house. Joyce placed her hands on brickwork which had been exposed as a result of this vandalism. She was staring into the distance but couldn't see very much. Terry was feeling her arse, his hands working their way into the waistband of her 501s.

'Take me this way,' Joyce instructed.

Terry unzipped the girl's jeans and pushed them down her legs. He got on his knees and took off the hippy's right sneaker. Joyce lifted her leg a few inches so that the denims could be eased over her foot. Since this enabled her to spread her legs as widely as they'd go, Blake didn't bother to free the Levis from around her left ankle. Terry shoved a hand between the girl's legs and brought his middle finger up against her clitoris.

Although Joyce couldn't see him, Winston was standing just a few hundred yards away. Ingliss was accompanied by a hand-picked commando of twenty-seven street-hardened men. Sixteen were soul brothers from the Sandringham Road area;

the rest constituted the membership of the Dalston Drop-outs – a multi-racial gang of anarcho-skins with a London-wide reputation for pig-bashing. The lads were receiving last-minute instructions before making an all-out attack on Hackney Police Station. Each was armed with a baseball bat. Winston and three trusted militants were also tooled up with shooters.

Terry worked his finger in and out of the hippy's love hole. Then he withdrew it altogether and stuck the digit in his mouth. He liked the taste. With his free hand, Blake unzipped his flies and took his prick out of his pants. He banged it a few times to stiffen it up.

'I want you to tear me apart with your big fat cock,' Joyce moaned.

The girl spread her legs while a few hundred yards away Winston's commando split into two groups. One to take the front of the police station and the other to assault the rear. After a three-minute count-down, the gang stormed the building.

'Taste the sweetness of destiny, racist pig!' a white skinhead screamed as he brought his baseball bat cracking against a desk sergeant's skull. There was the sickening crunch of splintering bone and the bastard staggered backwards before slumping to the ground. Then the boot-boy slammed a steel toe-capped DM into the copper's head. The latter quickly became a matted mess of blood and hair. The youth was making damn sure the scum-sucker was out of action.

'That feels so good,' Joyce squealed as Terry eased his fuck stick into her sex. She wriggled on the shaft like a speared fish and experienced a deathly ecstasy as it penetrated the very depths of her being.

Winston led the group taking the rear of the building. He'd left several men behind him to wipe out the opposition at ground level and gone running up the stairs to the next floor. He kicked open the door of the first room he came to. As he stormed the office a constable got up from behind a desk. Ingliss dropped his bat, grabbed the pig by the shirt and hurled this bloated example of anti-community relations head first through a window. The flesh on the bastard's forehead was torn open as he landed on a badly finished patch of concrete. Unfortunately, the PC felt little pain as he'd already blacked out.

Joyce was dimly aware of the sound of breaking glass and shouting but she was too far gone to take in their meaning. Terry was beating out the primitive rhythm of sex and the hippy was lost in this ecstasy. Blake was biting her neck, leaving marks on what he was beginning to perceive as his property.

Winston picked up his bat and sent it slamming against a skull belonging to one of the two coppers who'd come running into the room. A swift kick to the groin sent the second reeling backwards with his hands on his balls. The bastard was then knocked forward by another of his colleagues who'd hurried in behind him. The castration case fell to the floor with a yelp, while his comrade made a desperate attempt to regain his balance. Winston let fly with a fist and scored a direct hit on the cop's jaw. There was the usual satisfying crunch of breaking bone and the pig crashed to the ground spitting out gouts of blood and the occasional piece of broken tooth.

Terry was pumping up the volume as he worked Joyce towards orgasm. The boot-boy's thrusts were so hard that his balls were banging against the hippy's cunt. Blake had left Hackney and this vale of tears behind. He was in the full throes of a Near Death Experience.

The unexpectedness of their attack brought Winston's commando a swift victory. As his comrades scattered files across floors and smashed the canteen and toilets, Ingliss made his way down to the cells. He wasn't going to waste his time looking for keys, he'd simply shoot the locks off with his ·45. He aimed the gun and steadied it with both hands.

Terry knew he was about to come. He'd felt the love juice reach boiling-point inside his swollen manhood. His arms were bent around the girl's shoulders, and as he thrust upwards with his pelvis, he was using his hands to pull her bulk down on to his prick.

'Fuck me!' Joyce bellowed as Winston blew away the lock on the cell holding Freddie Love and three other soul brothers. Simultaneously, Blake offered up a wad of his genetic inheritance. An orgasm exploded in his brain and proceeded to ricochet through both his own bulk and that nominally belonging to the girl. Terry kept pumping as Ingliss shot the lock off every cell in the police station and thereby freed all the prisoners of conscience. Joyce was screaming her head off as multiple orgasms sent wave after wave of ecstasy surging through her bulk. Winston cleared the police station of both his commando and the men they'd rescued. Thanks to his skilled leadership, everything had gone according to plan.

Terry and Joyce leant against a mouldering wall and rasped obscenities at each other. Now that they'd satiated their lust, the overpowering smell of one hundred years of poverty was assailing their nostrils. Fat from thousands of cheap roasts had soaked into the plaster and only a total gutting would rid the building of this foul odour. Joyce was wondering how many people had fucked in the house. She tried to guess what proportion of its tenants had turned to drink in a vain attempt to escape grinding poverty. In her heart she knew that none of them ever really had the opportunity to make something of their lives. Poorly paid labouring and capitalist expropriation had condemned the so-called lower classes to the scrap-heap at birth.

For Terry, once you'd been in one Victorian terrace, you'd been in them all. Blake considered his high rise infinitely preferable to these vestiges of a fallen empire. If he ever drafted a political programme, destroying the structural remains of imperial Britain would be at the top of the agenda. While he reluctantly accepted the terrace as an architectural shell for shops and restaurants, he could not abide its use as housing. A people condemned to living in such conditions were likely to turn their backs on sexual ecstasy in favour of melancholia and Nordic mysticism.

What London needed was a fast, efficient and thoroughly modern system of public transportation. To this Terry wished to see added twenty-four-hour shopping, plenty of well-regarded but repetitive work and an architectural programme founded on something other than traditional red-brick designs. Such a pattern of reform would send the population into a sexual frenzy and cure at a swipe the British propensity for brooding. Instead of reproducing the introspective and oppressive culture that had been pioneered by Shakespeare, Wordsworth and Hardy, these islands would be integrated into the global ebb and flow of a communist potlatch.

'Come on,' Terry said as he adjusted his clothing. 'I'm sick of this place. Let's go.'

'I'm hungry,' Joyce said as she slipped her right leg back into her jeans.

'I need to pick something up from My One Flesh. We could go on from there to the Ridley Road Bagel Bakery,' Blake suggested.

Once Grant had retied the laces on her sneakers, the two polymorphs left the derelict terrace. Walking down Lower Clapton Road, Joyce was pleased to see the local nick had been wrecked. Two cops who'd just returned from a patrol in their Panda car were being comforted by ambulance men as their injured colleagues were carried out of the building. Terry expressed great pleasure at this state of affairs, despite being ignorant of its deeper significance.

'Alright, mate?' Blake greeted Raymond Nicolson as the pro-situ opened his front door.

'Very well, thank you,' the ex-public-school boy replied. 'Do come in.'

'I'm afraid I can't hang about,' Terry apologized. 'Have you got the dosh?'

'Yes, I'll just go and get it.'

Joyce was wondering what the hell was going on but decided it was best to leave the questions until later. Raymond returned with a very fully stuffed suitcase and handed it to Terry. The pro-situ was obviously tense about the whole deal.

'Don't worry, mate,' Blake said easily. 'I'll get you the warhead within a week.'

'I wouldn't be doing this if Rupert hadn't confirmed your claim. He says he's checked it against Debord's original French and the coded messages are definitely there. He's a bit pissed off that you spotted the cipher before him. Personally, I don't think it's such a big deal for Rupert. He isn't financing the operation. However, you've certainly convinced Rand that you're on to something. He threatened to disband My One Flesh if the membership refused to support this project.'

'Relax,' Terry said with a smile. 'Posterity will write your name into its book of revolutionary heroes.'

'It better!' the pro-situ shot back.

The two men exchanged goodbyes and Nicolson retreated into the house. Terry and Joyce walked several hundred yards in silence before the skinhead broke into maniacal laughter. He'd never quite believed he had the front to con these upper-class twits out of so much cash.

'What's the joke?' Joyce wanted to know.

'I persuaded those dickheads to give me a hundred thousand pounds so I could buy a nuclear bomb!' Blake said, exploding with laughter.

'So what are you gonna do?' the hippy demanded. 'Run off with the money?'

'They'll get their warhead, don't you worry.'

Joyce couldn't fathom Terry's mood. He was crazy enough to want to blow up London. On the other hand, she could see he'd have innumerable uses for the cash. In relation to all this, the hippy was certain of just one thing, which was that she wouldn't report the bomb threat to Seven. She wanted to have Blake's baby and so, dereliction of duty or not, she'd stick by him to the end.

The best thing you can say about the Ridley Road Bagel Bakery is that it stays open all night. Blake ordered teas and two cream-cheese bagels. The latter couldn't be compared to the ones sold in Brick Lane but they sufficed to line the stomach. Terry and Joyce sat on the suitcase and consumed their fare in the street.

'Fuck it,' Blake said. 'I'm sick of skimping on food. Let's go and get an Indian.'

'You buying?' Joyce asked.

'I can afford it,' the skinhead replied, tapping the suitcase.

Terry walked the few yards into Kingsland High Street and flagged down a cab. He called Joyce over and told the driver he wanted to go to the Sheba in Brick Lane. The cabbie managed to clip a Cortina on the corner of Calvert Avenue. Blake handed the man a tenner and told him to keep the change. It was quicker to walk than hang around until the accident was sorted out.

As they strolled through Arnold Circus, Terry spotted a graffitist hard at work. In letters more than a foot high, he'd written: SMASH CHRISTIANITY, SMASH ISLAM, NEITHER GOD NOR MASTER, ANARCHY IS FREEDOM, WE WELCOME RUSHDIE'S BLAS-PHEMY WHILE LOOKING FORWARD TO THIS BOURGEOIS WANKER'S DEATH AT THE HANDS OF A WORKING-CLASS MOB! Underneath, he was writing what was presumably the same text but in an Asian script. Terry clapped as the anarchist added the last character to his message. 'Right on mate!' Blake shouted. 'We're going to the Sheba – let me buy you dinner.'

'I'm Jackie Khan,' the youth said as he trotted over.

'I'm Terry Blake and this is Joyce Grant. Jackie can't be your real name.'

'It says Mohamed on my birth certificate, but despite breaking my mum's heart, I refuse to use it.'

'You left home?' Joyce asked.

'Sure,' Jackie replied. 'My folks kicked me out five years ago.'

'You're not that old!' the hippy exclaimed as she gave Jackie the once-over.

He grinned. 'I'm twenty-two.'

The conversation continued as they ambled along and seated themselves in the restaurant. Jackie explained how pissed off he got at whites who thought all asians were Muslim zealots. Personally, he had no time for religion and was heavily into sex, atheism and anarchy. Joyce said she thought there wasn't a culture in the world that didn't need freeing from the shackles of superstition. Terry chipped in by adding that Indian cooking pissed all over English cuisine.

After finishing their meal, they took a minicab to Joyce's flat on the Bow Bridge Estate. The hippy sat and watched as the two men kissed and felt each other up. Jackie said he didn't want to be fucked up the arse, so their intimacy went no further than petting. Eventually, Joyce stripped off and joined the bicycles fumbling with each other on her bed. Jackie lay flat on his back and the hippy took his cock in her mouth. She stuck her arse up in the air and Terry forced his head between her legs so that he could lick her out.

Once Joyce got really wet, she squatted over Jackie and eased his cock into her love hole. While the two of them beat out the primitive rhythm of sex, Blake lay to one side and played with himself.

After Grant had brought Khan to orgasm, she rolled over and guided Terry into the site of her mystery. Once he'd come, she sought further pleasures from Jackie. And so it went on all through the night.

Inspector Stephens surveyed the damage for the third time that morning. He was sick of hanging out in the Wimpy Bar which he'd transformed into a temporary HQ and decided to reoccupy the office he'd abandoned to a team of cleaners and repairmen. Just as the cop was about to order everyone out of the room, the phone rang.

'Hello,' he barked.

'Inspector Stephens?' a female voice inquired.

'Yes.'

'I'm Carol Inns from the *Daily Reporter*.'

'Look,' the policeman said gruffly, 'Telecom have only just reconnected the phone lines and I'm dealing with several urgent inquiries, so I'm afraid I'm not able to speak to you right now.'

'Is it true that you're a notorious racist?' the journalist persisted.

'Of course not,' the inspector replied irritably. 'Some of my best friends are Irish.'

'I wasn't intending to ask you about your connections with Loyalist paramilitary groups, but since you've brought up the subject . . .'

'I've told you, I'm too busy to answer any questions. You'll just have to wait for a press statement.' The cop slammed down the phone before the reporter had time to reply.

When the phone rang again, the inspector instructed a PC to answer it and inform the caller he was busy. Stephens felt both traumatized and humiliated – dealing with aggressive outsiders was the last thing he wanted to do while he was still trying to collect his wits.

'Jim!' Arthur Roberts boomed as he walked into the room. 'I've been trying to find you all morning. What the fuck's going on?'

'Don't mock me!' the cop brayed. 'You know as well as I do that last night a bunch of colonials ransacked my police station. Their vendetta against the white man is the product of jealousy and genetic self-hatred. Confronted with the greatness of a civilization against which scientists can measure their biological inferiority, these apes resort to jungle savagery and other antics from the Dark Ages!'

'But some of the youths were white,' Roberts protested, 'and I'd wager all of them were born here.'

'Liberal cant!' Stephens bellowed. 'There weren't any whites in the gang, only blacks and race traitors!'

'I've told you before,' the anti-racist said coldly, 'if these are your views, you should keep them to yourself. By airing them in public you'll bring your uniform into disrepute. There's no room in our multicultural society for public servants who want to see a return to policies which were abandoned with the fall of the Empire.'

'I'm upset,' the inspector replied by way of defence. 'Last night three of my men were murdered in cold blood and another eleven hospitalized.'

'I understand that you feel out of sorts,' Roberts sympathized, 'but as a policeman you have to learn to keep your feelings hidden under a cloak of professionalism.'

'You're right,' his colleague hissed. 'Now let's get down to business.'

'I understand that all the prisoners escaped last night.'

'They were sprung,' the cop corrected.

'Well,' Roberts said, 'I've gotta have someone to execute in your cells. You'll just have to go out and arrest the first black you can find. I'll do the rest.'

'But we don't need the riot any more,' Stephens protested. 'This unprovoked assault on my police station is reason enough to institute martial law.'

'I've briefed several score of communist cadres to pose as fascist *provocateurs* during this evening's disturbances. It's too late for me to reach them all and call off the manoeuvre. There has to be a riot tonight!'

Roberts sat behind the inspector's desk while the policeman went looking for someone to pull in. The spymaster opened the latest issue of *Highlight*, the *Anti-Racist Monthly*. He wanted to check out what the opposition were saying. These bastards had been encroaching on his territory for years, but with a little bit of luck he'd eventually swing things so that they went out of business.

'I've got one in the cells,' Stephens said cheerfully as he came back into the room.

'Christ,' Roberts swore, 'that was quick.'

'She was walking past the station as I went out – a real stroke of luck.'

'I'll deal with this alone,' the anti-fascist told his uniformed junior.

'There's a padlock on the cell,' the inspector explained as he handed Roberts a key. 'It's a temporary measure until the mortice is fixed. All the locks were shot to fuck last night.'

The anti-fascist was aware of the ·45 pressing against his armpit. On becoming politically active, Roberts had accepted that duty inevitably accompanied ideological commitment. This wasn't the first unpleasant task that had been forced upon him in the pursuit of a noble cause. It was, he reflected as he opened the cell door, a regrettable necessity which was driving him to shoot one of his black sisters.

'Arthur!' the prisoner whooped as she jumped up and flung her arms around him. 'I haven't seen you since the day we both graduated from college.'

Roberts was thrown into a deep confusion as Dorothy Butler kissed him passionately. Stephens had pulled in a woman with whom the anti-fascist had enjoyed a torrid affair while still an undergraduate. His old man had threatened to cut him off without a penny if the relationship continued after he left university. Until his death, Roberts senior had blamed Dorothy for awakening in Arthur an unnatural interest in the coloured question. His mother, who was more severe in her judgements, had viewed Dolly as a temporary appendage which her son flaunted as a sign of his youthful rebellion and exotic tastes. Ma Roberts, who'd grown bitter about the way she was shown off to her husband's business associates, felt sick to the stomach every time she heard her eldest child boasting about his beautiful black girl-friend.

The years had not been kind to Dorothy. After her husband ran off with her best friend, and six months later her only child was killed in a hit-and-run accident, she'd taken to drink. Butler had bloated to three times the size she'd been when Roberts last saw her. Dolly's clothes were ragged and she needed a bath. The anti-fascist found it hard to believe that he'd once been sexually attracted to this woman. Nevertheless, he did not feel up to the task of shooting her in cold blood.

'I'm doing some research into institutionalized racism amongst the police,' Roberts lied.

'I've followed your career,' his old flame replied, 'and I've always felt so proud to have known you. You've remained so uncompromising, championing the poor and oppressed, when you could have been earning a mint from your family connections.'

Roberts wanted to cry. He found this woman's belief in him completely humiliating. Butler was right when she said she'd followed his career – that was all it was. His anti-racism had begun as high-spirited teenage rebellion and soon become no more than a routine occupation. Having confronted him with Dorothy, fate had forced Roberts to admit he was the very worst kind of fake. Now he was desperate to get this woman out of his life before she ruined him.

'Come on,' the anti-fascist said, 'I'll take you home.'

Dolly directed Roberts to Sandringham Road. He'd intended to drop her off and drive away. However, Butler insisted that her old boy-friend park the car and stop for a cup of tea. As a second pot was brewing, Dorothy told her teenage sweetheart she wanted to make love to him, just for old time's sake. The anti-fascist felt unable to refuse this request despite finding the very idea of sex with Dolly nauseating. He knew that afterwards he'd become morbidly obsessed with the filthy bandage tied round the hag's right calf. Roberts hoped this revulsion wasn't simply a reaction to the ungraceful way in which Dorothy had ballooned into middle age. Going beyond physical appearances, he felt himself spiritually inferior to this broken alcoholic. What he needed was a selfish bitch like Joyce Grant, a little slut who was his moral inferior.

In pursuit of penetration, Roberts had to fight his way through several rolls of fat. When he finally reached his objective, he made a couple of thrusts and then shot off a wad of liquid genetics. An unsympathetic observer might have argued that the anti-fascist's orgasm was little more than a premature ejaculation. Roberts kissed Dolly and then crawled to the toilet, where he threw up.

'Poor baby!' Dorothy cried when she realized he'd been sick.

She led Arthur back to bed and tucked him beneath the sheets. Dolly handed Roberts a bottle of whisky and the anti-fascist gulped down several mouthfuls of this medicine. He had a light fever and was aching to get some sleep. His old flame put her hand on his forehead and spoke to him in a soothing voice. By closing his eyes, the anti-fascist was able to imagine that Dorothy hadn't changed since she'd been his teenage sweetheart. In the early sixties there'd been a whole world for Arthur to win.

Roberts tossed and turned throughout the afternoon. He slept fitfully and, every time he opened his eyes, the light sent a searing pain into the furthermost depths of his cortex.

Now it was dusk and a dull ache had settled on his bones. The anti-fascist couldn't identify the noises coming from the street but knew he was somehow connected to them:

> 'Comrades! The voices of the dead battalions
> Of those who fell
> That Britain might be Great;
> Join in our song,
> For they march in spirit with us and urge us on,
> To build the people's state.'

The élite communist cadres who'd been hand-picked by Roberts to pose as fascist *provocateurs* were marching along Sandringham Road singing the 'English Horst Wessel'. They were somewhat bemused by the fact that all the dope-peddlers had disappeared from Hackney's Front Line. Their singing didn't appear to upset anyone, but in their lemming-like commitment to Leninist ideals, the anti-fascists felt it best to obey the letter of their orders.

> 'Blood of their blood, and spirit of their spirit;
> Sprung from the soil
> For whose dear sake they bled;
> 'Gainst Jewish power, Red Front and mad dogs of Reaction
> We will lead the fight
> For Freedom and for Bread.'

As the hundred-strong phalanx of communists reached the top of Sandringham Road and turned round, seven members of Cockney Nation joined their ranks. Having discovered one hundred political soldiers bellowing out this Brownshirt marching song, the Third Positionists were eager to grab a slice of the action.

> 'The streets are still, the final battle's ended,
> Flushed with the fight,
> We proudly hail the dawn.
> See over all the streets, the Union Jack is waving,
> Triumphant standard
> Of a race reborn.'

Arthur Roberts was asleep in Dolly's flat but the sounds from the street wove themselves into his dreams. Next to a burning cross stood a sinister figure dressed in a white hood and the robes of an Imperial Wizard of the Ku-Klux-Klan. The racist turned and fled as hundreds of communists marched towards him.

The cadres Roberts had chosen to pose as fascist *provocateurs* were selected on the basis of their unquestioning loyalty to the Leninist cause. To find the right calibre of zealot, the anti-fascist had picked individuals from groups and sections located all over London and the Home Counties. This led to a fatal weakness among the troops. If there was a fight, the majority of the cadres had no means of telling friend from foe.

As the song had come to an end, the membership of Cockney Nation bellowed out the first verse again. About half the rank joined in, but several Leninists who'd been at the rear of the troop turned round and accused the Third Positionists of being Nazis. 'We're left-wing fascists,' one among their number cried defensively. 'We defend the doctrines elaborated by the Strasser brothers and have nothing but contempt for the bourgeoisie and their Hitlerite creeds. We're White Nationalist Revolutionaries!'

At this point, a Leninist stepped forward and smashed his fist into the Third Positionist's mouth. There was the satisfying crunch of splintering bone and the bastard staggered backwards spitting out gouts of blood and the occasional piece of broken tooth. This incident acted as a trigger for fighting to break out up and down the column of shock-troops. While the fascists who'd joined the rear of the march received a good kicking, elsewhere comrades were fighting it out with comrades who they wrongly imagined to be Nazi scum.

It was at this point that Alan Anger and Pete Wild arrived in Sandringham Road. They'd been hoping to score some dope. When they saw the massed ranks of fascists beating shit out of each other, they jumped for joy. Once they'd got some reinforcements, they'd come back for a spot of Nazi-bashing. The teenagers had anarchist parents and so bigot-baiting had been a family activity since their earliest childhood.

It was Raymond who answered the door when the two youths called on the My One Flesh HQ in Graham Road. The pro-situ led them into the living-room where Rupert Dawson-Rand was leading a political discussion. 'Come on,' the boys were shouting, 'let's go and 'ave the Nazis!'

Arnold immediately put on his coat and said he'd drive everybody up to the front line. It was only a few minutes' walk but it'd be even faster in a car. Rodney, Raymond and Sebastian were less enthusiastic but agreed to go.

'I don't think the caviare I had for lunch has settled too well,' Rupert whimpered as he jumped up and ran to the toilet.

Actually, it wasn't his dinner that was causing the pro-situ to shit himself, but no one else was in a position to prove this. By the time the rest of the crew got up to Sandringham Road, they'd missed the best of the violence. The Leninist impostors and the membership of Cockney Nation were littering the street. Already their wallets had been lifted by quick-thinking soul brothers. The pro-situs drove their car over a few of the fascist wankers before turning round to go home.

Roberts was still dreaming in Dolly's flat. His faithful Leninist cadres had caught up with the white-robed racist. When they removed the scumbag's hood, the anti-fascist was horrified to see his own face. Nevertheless, he spat defiantly at his own followers when they accused him of being a traitor.

Eight

When the planners dreamt up Crisp Street, they hailed it as a Utopian vision of how the British would shop in the future. It might have been the country's first purpose-built pedestrian market, but forty years after the event, rather than being the paradise the architects had promised, it appeared more like hell on earth to the people of Poplar.

Joyce and Jackie were standing opposite the snack-stall when Terry arrived. They were drinking tea and chewing on cheese sandwiches. Blake bought himself a coffee before joining them. After a brief discussion they decided to walk to Canning Town rather than hang around for a bus. As they ambled out of the market, Jackie noticed fascist graffiti painted on the corner of Crisp and Willis Streets. EAST LONDON A NATION, it proclaimed. Khan took a spray-can from his carrier, crossed out EAST LONDON and wrote Q: TEVIOT above the letters he'd obliterated, then added a question mark after the word NATION. Underneath he provided the solution to this riddle: A: THE WORKING CLASS HAS NO COUNTRY.

Terry had to laugh. These political messages were so out of place. The gang from the Teviot Estate and their opposite numbers on the Isle of Dogs had been feuding for years. These rivals had sprayed graffiti, informing the world of their mutual hatred, over thousands of walls in the area. There were hundreds of I.O.D. KILLS TEVIOT and vice-versa slogans, as well as a few gang classics, to be found in the neighbourhood. Blake's personal favourite was still the ancient and partly faded WARNING: YOU ARE NOW ENTERING TEVIOT. However, this sectarian admonishment held pride of place only by default. East London's most famous piece of graffiti had nothing to do with gang warfare. It had been painted on a wall that the developers bulldozed as one of their many contributions to Docklands development. Under a sign welcoming visitors to the Isle of Dogs were the instructions LOOT ASDA, BURN BARRATS. Despite George Lansbury and the pre-war Councillors' Revolt, political graffiti was still a rare phenomenon in *Red* Poplar. This was why Jackie's intervention raised a horse laugh from Terry.

Strolling along the East India Dock Road to Canning Town as the traffic thunders by isn't a particularly pleasant way to pass an afternoon. Fortunately, you can cover the distance from Poplar in ten or fifteen minutes. The Third Positionists lived at the western end of the Barking Road. Opposite their flat was more fascist graffiti. ULSTER A NATION, it proclaimed, alongside a repeat of the slogan Jackie had altered in Crisp Street.

'Alright mate?' Terry said to the rather battered-looking fascist who opened the door. 'I've got the medical gear you need to carry out the blood-tests.'

'Pride in your own kind, respect for others,' Jackie said to the Brownshirt as he walked in behind Blake.

'Hi,' Joyce said as she brought up the rear.

Blake was sickened by the dirt that had been allowed to accumulate inside the flat. The Third Positionists lived like the pigs they undoubtedly were. Scum-suckers who couldn't even be bothered to clean their own home. There were various flags belonging to the so-called British Family of Nations decorating the walls, alongside posters advertising product by Skrewdriver and Skullhead. Terry liked the music of both these skinhead bands, and the lyrics of the latter never failed to have him rolling on the floor. The all-time classic was 'Blame the Bosses', in which singer Kev Turner claimed that 'the blacks' were a 'capitalist creation'. In his earnest desire to embrace the Third Position, Turner tried to mix his bigoted views with a touch of undigested Marxism, and the result was some of the best unintentional humour since William MacGonagal last tramped the streets of Dundee.

'Tom and Keith, this is Joyce and this is Jackie,' Blake said, making the introductions.

'Hello,' the bigots replied in unison.

'What happened to you?' Terry asked. 'You both look as if you've been run over by a bus.'

'We got in a ruck with a bunch of commie scum,' Tom explained. 'They outnumbered us, but we sorted the cowards out in the end. Me and Keith were lucky – three of our comrades had to be rushed into intensive care after some Red bastard drove over them in a car.'

'Where are you from?' Jackie asked, after spotting an unmistakable Northern twang in the speaker's voice.

'We're both from Leeds,' Keith explained. 'We moved to London about a year ago after we'd traced back our respective family trees. My ancestors went north from Poplar in about the sixth century. Tom's left Aldgate in 1822.'

'But Poplar didn't exist in the sixth century!' Terry protested.

'Yes, it did!' Tom retorted. 'You've been taken in by the conspiracy. The Cockney Nation has existed for millions of years. It's just that the Jews have obscured this fact by falsifying the entire history of the world prior to 1945.'

'How do you know there's a conspiracy?' Jackie demanded.

'It's obvious,' Keith replied. 'There's no other way in which you can explain the train of world events which have led to the near-collapse of white civilization. However, we're not only witnessing the decline of everything the Cockney holds dear – your Indian culture is being destroyed too.'

'But I was born in London,' Khan protested.

'That's not the point,' Tom explained patiently. 'If it wasn't for the Zionists, you'd have been born into a unique Indian culture instead of this multiracial nightmare.'

'You see,' Keith went on, 'the Jews are foisting multiculturalism on all other races, while as a people they stubbornly resist assimilation! If you don't believe me, look at the number of Semites promoting race-mixing within the socialist movement and then study the pronouncements of their rabbis on the question of race.'

'Hang on a minute!' Jackie protested. 'You're confusing two sets of people. Progressives like Marx and Trotsky were atheists whose socialism led them to oppose all racial divisions while attempting to organize the masses internationally on a class basis. They'd made a complete break with the rabbis and other reactionaries. There's absolutely no connection between the socialists who promote working-class internationalism and the old guard of religious bigots!'

'Yes, there is,' Tom retorted. 'They're all Jewish!'

'It's not worth arguing with you,' Jackie snorted.

'You see,' Tom replied, 'we win every discussion we have with our opponents because Cockney Nation has made a full study of political ideology. We're not going to be browbeaten with Marxist hogwash!'

'What the fuck do you mean by Ulster Nation?' Joyce demanded, hoping that this question would alter the course of the conversation.

'That Northern Ireland is historically an independent territory within the British Family of Nations,' Keith replied smugly.

'So by Ulster you mean the six counties of Northern Ireland,' Joyce persisted.

'There are only six counties in Northern Ireland,' Tom snapped.

'Yes,' Joyce agreed, 'but the historic kingdom of Ulster is made up of nine counties, three of which are located in the Republic.'

'Eh?' Tom and Keith replied in unison. 'We've never heard about this.'

'That's because you're so bleedin' ignorant you don't even know when you've lost an argument,' Joyce hissed.

'No, it's not!' Keith screamed indignantly. 'This nine counties nonsense must be something put about by the conspiracy. It has to be – neither Tom nor I have ever heard of it.'

'Look,' Terry put in, 'why don't we call a halt to this political debate. I came here to pass on the blood-testing gear for a trifling remuneration.'

'You sort out your business,' Joyce spat. 'Jackie and me are going through to the kitchen to make tea.'

'Good idea,' Tom said. 'Making refreshments is one of the few things women are good for.'

Khan followed the hippy out of the room. He watched as she boiled water and warmed the pot, then spooned in tea before adding something from one of those self-sealing plastic bags in which spaceheads stash their dope.

'Powdered magic mushrooms,' Joyce whispered. 'I wanna see how those fascists deal with a touch of cosmic ecstasy.'

Terry'd got the five hundred quid off the Third Positionists by the time Joyce and Jackie emerged from the kitchen with the tea. He'd wormed his way out of providing a detailed explanation of how to use the medical gear by thrusting twenty pages of Xeroxes into Tom's hand.

'Tea everybody?' Joyce asked.

'No,' Blake replied as he got up and walked through to the kitchen. 'I'm gonna get myself a coffee.'

Terry was disgusted to find the Brownshirts only had Nescafé. Keith and Tom had destroyed their palates with years of heavy smoking. They didn't notice that the tea Joyce served up tasted a little strange and both the bigots drank a second cup.

'You see,' Keith was pontificating, 'we need to provide the courts with sentences which are a real deterrent to the criminally inclined. That's why our soon to be installed National Socialist government will reintroduce capital punishment. Repatriation will put an end to much violent crime, but among young whites there'll still be a terrible drugs problem. However, pushers will think twice before carrying on their trade if they know there's a serious possibility of being hung for their antisocial activities.'

'Have you ever done drugs yourself?' Joyce inquired.

'Of course not!' Keith snorted.

'You will have soon because I spiked your tea.'

'What!' the fascist cried as he lunged at the hippy.

'I wouldn't touch her if I was you,' Jackie advised as he pushed the Brownshirt back into his seat. 'If it's the first time you've done a hallucinogenic, you'll need Joyce to guide you through the trip.'

'There's giant spiders crawling up the walls!' Tom screamed maniacally.

'Don't be ridiculous,' Joyce snapped, 'the mushrooms haven't had time to take effect. There's a time-lag of at least thirty minutes between ingestion and the psycho-active agents working their way through the bloodstream and into the brain.'

'Spiders, spiders!' the fascist repeated as he foamed at the mouth.

'You've gone mental,' Terry said coldly. 'There's nothing there.'

Tom jumped up from his seat and ran out of the flat. A minute later there was a blaring of horns and a squealing of brakes. Keith, Joyce, Jackie and Terry raced to the window. Outside, they could see the Brownshirt's splattered remains spread across the Barking Road. Keith froze and it took a great deal of pushing and shoving to manoeuvre him into a chair. He'd slipped into a catatonic trance and it was only when wailing sirens announced the arrival of police cars and an ambulance that the Third Positionist was able to give upfront expression to his feelings of grief, which took the form of uncontrolled sobbing.

'You stay here,' Blake told Khan. 'Me and Joyce are gonna take this wanker for a walk.'

The hippy looked quizzically at Terry but decided not to question what he was doing. The mushrooms were beginning to take effect and she'd become temporarily incapable of constituting herself as a bourgeois subject possessed by strong leadership qualities. However, once they were out in the street, Grant did manage to insist that the three of them visit a tobacconist.

'Packet of skins please.' Joyce felt like she had the words MAGIC MUSHROOMS stamped in bold letters on her forehead. 'Ooops, I mean Rizlas.'

Back at the flat, Khan was imagining that he'd just witnessed a secret reunion concert by the Doors. Jim Morrison had faked his own death and split for Africa. But in the world's hour of need, this rock star had re-formed his group to play live for a select band of militants. The ballroom emptied and soon afterwards Jackie had changed sex – he was now a woman. Mist swirled around him as he drifted across the dance floor. A telephone was ringing and the waves of sound were rolling across the room and crushing the young anarchist. Khan thought he was going to die, but fortunately the caller hung up and he was spared any further pain.

'You see,' Terry was explaining to Keith, 'here in the future we don't have a problem with racists because the old peoples of the world interbred to such an extent that it's no longer possible to distinguish between them. We're all coffee-coloured now. I say all, but there were a handful of Nordic types who objected to this process and retreated to the Highlands of Scotland. Nobody saw them for hundreds of years, and during this time they inbred and thoroughly poisoned their gene pool. Their subhuman descendants came out from the hills a few years ago and begged us to provide them with food and shelter. These degenerates are an evolutionary abortion, they're incapable of fending for themselves. We built a home for them here in London and I've brought you to see the last remaining white men.'

Blake had actually led Keith and Joyce into a building that housed a play scheme for mentally handicapped teenagers. However, the Third Positionist was too bombed out to realize this and gaped in horror at what he believed to be the last specimens of the once mighty white race. Terry's little story brought home to the bigot exactly what the outcome of his race-hate theories would be, if anyone ever got the chance to put them into practice. A refusal to bring new blood into any community will swiftly result in degeneration and ultimately idiocy. The fascist felt a cloud of depression descend upon him. All his years of political activism had been in the service of a cause that could never win. If the race-mixers didn't beat the bigots, then the racists would defeat themselves.

Back at the flat, darkness had descended upon Jackie. Somehow he'd been reduced to a height of one centimetre and become trapped inside his own mind. He was stuck inside a void. He could not see, feel, hear, taste or smell. This was a form of sensory deprivation more total than anything that could be imposed upon him by an experimental psychologist and it caused the young anarchist to lose all sense of time. Eventually he heard Joyce, Keith and Terry trooping up the stairs and into the flat.

'What's wrong, Jack?' Terry demanded as he shook the anarchist's bulk.

Khan tried to reply, but it soon became apparent that Blake couldn't hear him. It was like awakening from a nightmare and being menaced by terrors far worse than those faced during sleep. Jackie was conscious but unable to communicate this to his comrades. Khan heard Joyce phone for an ambulance, and the efforts he made to open his mouth and scream that she shouldn't do this proved futile. He was aware of being loaded onto a stretcher and driven to hospital – all without being able to tell those caring for him that he was trapped inside his own mind. Khan didn't know how long he'd been lying in an NHS bed, but the authorities had managed to fetch his mother from Southall.

'I never thought he'd be so stupid,' she was wailing to the doctor. 'He was always troublesome, but I can't believe he turned to drugs.'

Terry wasn't worrying about Keith. He seemed to have come down enough to take care of himself. The fascist fumbled with his keys and opened the door to his flat without undue effort. Joyce was the first to notice Khan, who was sprawled in a heap on the floor.

'Are you OK?' Grant asked as she rolled Jackie on to his back.

'Christ,' the boy said as he blinked up at her, 'have I had a bad trip.'

Terry made coffee. Having sobered up with a cup of java, the comrades left Keith brooding in his flat. They made their way back to the hippy's pad on the Bow Bridge Estate, where Winston Ingliss was waiting for them. This select band of militants were finalizing their plans for a riot they'd scheduled to take place later that week. In just over forty-eight hours, Westminster would explode in an orgy of premeditated violence. Meanwhile, the Third Positionist received a most unwelcome phone call.

'Keith, it's Brian. I've just got wind of what the United Britons Party are planning. In two days time they're gonna march down Sandringham Road. As you know, these reactionary bigots are always trying to muscle in on our territory. Cockney Nation has to oppose these wankers and so I've arranged a counter-demonstration. The Brixton Black Separatists have agreed to come along to support us. However, I've some bad news on the numbers front. John, Tony and Derek all died in Homerton Hospital last night. As you no doubt realize, their loss means that we no longer have a large enough membership to make Cockney Nation viable as a political organization. Therefore, I've no choice but to begin merger negotiations with Harold Denmark's mob. . . . Keith, Keith? Are you there, Keith? Look, it isn't as bad as all that. I won't agree to anything until they accept that Cockney Nation must be treated as an autonomous state within a future federated Britain. Keith, speak to me. . . .'

Coming down the telephone line, Brian Smith could hear the sound of glass shattering. Keith had jumped through the front window of his Newham flat. There was the sickening crunch of splintering bone as the stretcher-case landed head first on the pavement. The Brownshirt had done the decent thing, Smith reflected as he hung up. In Brian's book, nationalists unable to meet the exacting demands of spiritual revolution were honour bound to take their lives. No one could live honourably once they'd faltered in their duties as a patriot.

Maintaining his natural inclination towards lofty thought but bringing his mind to bear on matters in hand, the Führer of

Cockney Nation made a realistic assessment of the situation and concluded that his movement was finished. This most daring experiment in nationalist politics had been aborted just before noon by no less eminent a figure than Arthur J. Roberts, a man famed for the crusade he'd waged against extremists of every stripe. The Mr Fix-It of counter-subversion had phoned Smith and told him of the deaths at Homerton Hospital, before instructing this fascist hireling to begin merger negotiations with Harold Denmark's Third Position. The man from Seven cruelly insisted that with a membership of four, Cockney Nation was no longer a viable proposition. Brian, eager to retain his state patronage, had reluctantly agreed to his controller's proposals for realigning the forces of the far-Right. Immediately afterwards, he'd called his old rival and offered him the open hand of reconciliation. After a tense conversation, what finally clinched a meeting at The Lamb was the offer of hard cash if the two grouplets could find a way of working together.

Nazi Pat and Plaistow Tim responded with abuse when it was put to them that Cockney Nation should try working with members of Denmark's Third Position. Thirty minutes later, they phoned Brian and advised him that, should he seek to join their newly formed tendency, Newham Forever, his application would be turned down. Worse still, these ungrateful turncoats suggested that Smith was a stooge of the conspiracy who would free Newham from the domination of Westminster only to crush the spirit of its people under the weight of a foreign bureaucracy who owed their allegiance to Hackney. Cockney Nation, they asserted, was the dream of an imperialistic power. Furthermore, they would not stand idly by while Newham was trampled underfoot by a succession of alien usurpers. They were going to smash the power of the political bosses who'd destroyed thousands of nations in their greed for profit. Newham Forever had seen through the lies put about by the likes of Smith and Denmark. Although reactionaries of this type draped themselves in the colours of National Liberation, they were actually the very worst kind of capitalist scum! In the face of this threat, Newham Forever would quickly grow into a mass movement whose initials were scrawled across a thousand East London walls. The NF partisans would liquidate Smith and Denmark along with the rest of the leeches who sucked at the very life-blood of their nation.

'I'll see that you're blackballed from the far-Right,' Brian hissed into his receiver.

'Traitor!' Pat squawked. 'Newham Forever is seeking a Third Way beyond capitalism and communism. We don't give a shit about the far-Right. You and your bigoted mates are no better than the Reds. Those whose judge you perhaps imagine yourself to be, will one day judge you. We shall be waiting for you at the turning!'

'You'll never defeat me,' Smith spat. 'You don't even have a theoretical grasp of how to apply the hammer-blow of *putsch*, let alone the ability to attempt a practical realization of this deadly tactic. I'm expelling the pair of you from Cockney Nation. And be warned, I'll have you hanged on the day I lead the glorious forces of nationalism to victory. You're just a pair of loonies. Launching an independence movement to liberate Newham is gonna make you a laughing-stock among sincere patriots.'

'Fuck off!' Pat swore as he slammed down his receiver.

Brian was exhilarated by this clash of wills. He was rightly proud of the ease with which he'd put down the opposition. His skilful deployment of rhetoric was an accomplishment that not even his worst enemies could belittle! The encounter had amply demonstrated his intellectual skills and shown to full advantage his natural bent for leadership.

Smith checked his watch and found he had an hour to kill. Even London Transport was capable of getting him to Holborn in less than forty-five minutes. The Third Positionist wanted to relax before heading off to the rendezvous with Denmark. Hidden behind his collection of Wagner and Walton recordings was a Boney M compilation album. The fascist slapped the pop platter on his deck. After donning a set of headphones, he abandoned himself to the beat. This true-blue patriot didn't dare listen to the disc through the main speaker system. To do so was to risk flushing his political career down the toilet. Before embracing the Third Position, Smith had regularly decried the malign influence of degenerate negroid rhythms on all European popular music composed since the First World War. While Brian no longer publicly foamed at the mouth while ranting about Aryan superiority, it would not do to be caught listening to the bastard offspring of musical miscegenation.

The fascist closed his eyes, slumped back in an easy chair and let his hand move over his crotch. The repetitive beat sent him into a trance. He unzipped his flies, took his cock out and began to massage the love muscle. Smith imagined that rather than being in Hackney, he was addressing a secret meeting of Third Position militants at a top West End hotel:

'Having established our *modus agendi*, we will occupy ourselves with the details of those combinations by which we will complete the revolution of the machinery of state in the direction I've already indicated. By these combinations, I mean freedom of the press, the right of association, freedom of conscience, the voting principle, and many another which must disappear for ever from the memory of our people, or undergo a radical alteration the day after the promulgation of our Third Positionist constitution.'

As the needle hit the second track on the album, which belted along at a higher rate of beats per minute than the first, the speed with which Smith worked his length increased.

'It is at this moment that we shall announce all our orders, for afterwards every noticeable alteration will be counter-productive. If the New Reich is ushered in with harsh severity and engenders an atmosphere of resignation caused by feelings of foreboding, it will lead to a general attitude of hopelessness and deference to our rule.'

The fascist's breathing was heavy. He was massaging his love muscle in a steady and monotonous pulse. This was the beat of consumer society, the rhythm of the factory, which when reproduced in the proletariat led to a delightful sexual stupor. It was a soporific that simultaneously induced feelings of security and ecstatic loss of self in an orgy of sensual indulgence. What reactionary wankers like Smith failed to realize was that ultimately these feelings would overthrow the order of production by providing a direct challenge to the hegemony of bourgeois culture. This was an order Smith supported in everything but name.

'Nothing must be injurious to the prestige of our New Order. I desire that from the moment it achieves power, while the multiracial melting-pot is still stunned by the accomplished fact of National Revolution, still in a condition of terror and uncertainty, that the masses should recognize once and for all that I am so strong that I've no need to pretend to take account of their wishes. In fact, far from paying any attention to the opinions of masses, I'm ready and able to crush with irresistible force those treacherous elements which would rise up against me.'

The Third Positionist could feel his genetic wealth boiling up through his penis while a tidal wave of endorphins flooded his brain. Surely no one would deny that it was through a sexual revolution that the élite would achieve a militant dictatorship of the spirit!

'After installing a National Socialist government I will promise the masses that they'll get back all the liberties they've had taken away as soon as I've quelled the enemies of peace and tamed all parties. However, I'll refuse to discuss with them how long they'll be kept waiting for the return of their rights as free citizens.'

As he completed his speech, Smith shot a wad of come across the room and it splattered over a picture of a topless model who was gracing page three of a well-known tabloid newspaper. The Third Positionist sunk even further into his chair and the music of Boney M lulled him into a deep and relaxing sleep.

Smith dozed for twenty minutes, then roused himself and headed for Holborn. Denmark was hidden behind one of the glass snob screens which the owners of the Lamb had installed around the bar in the 1960s. Once Smith and his old rival were armed with pints, they retired to a corner of the pub.

'So why do you want a merger?' the Führer of Third Position demanded.

'You've got the membership, I've got the money,' Smith replied. 'As you know, most of my cadres lived in Newham. They were a bunch of malcontents who objected to their leader being based in Hackney. I've expelled the lot of 'em!'

'Are you telling me that it's only you, and not your cadres, wanting to join Third Position?'

'Once this Newham Forever nonsense blows over, I'm sure most of the members will follow my lead and enlist in your ranks. In the meantime, I constitute the entire membership of Cockney Nation. Everyone else has been expelled.'

'That doesn't put you in a very strong bargaining position.'

'I've got plenty to offer you,' Smith hissed. 'Enough money to finance a theoretical monthly and a street paper.'

'We're already publishing these things without any outside aid,' Denmark retorted.

'Yes,' Smith laughed. 'Three wafer-thin issues of *Nationalist Monthly* in the past year, while *Third Position News* still doesn't hit the streets as often as it should.'

'OK, so we could use the money. How much is there and where is it coming from?'

'Twelve thousand a year, paid in monthly instalments, on the condition that every last penny of it is used to subsidize publications.'

'These are my terms,' Denmark replied as he made a quick calculation of the degree to which he could humiliate Smith and still get his hands on the old codger's dosh. 'We need the money as non-returnable cash donations. After we've received the first payment, you can work alongside Third Position. If you show the necessary commitment over a period of six months, we'll let you take out a subscription as a Friend of the Movement. After that, you can apply for cadre status in the normal way.'

'Are you saying I have to wait a year and then sit exams which test my understanding of your political ideology?' Smith wailed.

'Take it or leave it,' the younger man snapped.

'It's a deal,' Smith said, holding out his hand.

'One other thing,' Denmark insisted. 'You have to tell me where the money comes from.'

'Bank robberies,' came the completely deadpan reply.

Anti-Fascist Probe regularly circulated reports to the effect that Cockney Nation was financed from the proceeds of armed villainy. Denmark had always dismissed these claims as little more than communist and/or Special Branch lies. He was, however, in no position to quibble with the factual accuracy of the information if the former leader of Cockney Nation claimed it was true. Denmark was desperate for the dosh Brian Smith had offered him and wasn't overly concerned if it was the product of criminal, or other dubious, activities. He would have willingly accepted money from anyone, even Arthur Roberts or some other agent of the British security services.

Nine

'Hi, remember me from last night?' the girl said as she shook Terry awake. 'I have to go soon, so let's just have a ten-minute session. Hang on while I set the alarm. I've got a very important meeting this morning!'

Blake racked his brain and tried to remember where he'd met the brown-haired raver. Both this and the girl's name escaped him. The details didn't matter – waking up in the arms of a stranger had long been a daily occurrence in the life of the sexed-up skinhead.

'Ten,' the girl panted after Blake had been beating out the primitive rhythm of the swamps for nine minutes and fifty seconds. 'Eight, seven. . . .'

Terry could feel liquid genetics boiling in his groin. The way the brunette thundered through the countdown left her partner in no doubt about the fact that she was fast approaching orgasm, and knowledge of this greatly fuelled Blake's excitement. The current of sexual energy that was charging these male and female poles would soon short circuit into an endorphin-soaked explosion of carnal delight.

'Three, two, ONE!' the girl bellowed.

A tidal wave of an orgasm crashed through the twin bulks that had been thrashing on the bed. Simultaneously, Terry's alarm began to emit a series of angry bleeps. The noise cut through the skinhead's brain like a butcher's cleaver slicing up meat. Blake slammed a palm against the top of his clock. The brunette gave herself three minutes to recover, then pushed Terry from her chest, got up from the bed, washed and dressed. She kissed the boot-boy goodbye and was gone.

Blake dozed for fifty minutes before getting up. He gobbled two slices of toast, drank a very strong coffee, grabbed his Walkman and strode purposefully to Crossharbour Station. The boot-boy needed a good day's shopping to lift the cloud of depression that had settled on his mind. He was disturbed by the extent to which he'd become involved with Joyce. Despite all the casual sex, Terry'd remained a lone wolf since breaking up with Heather nearly ten years ago. He couldn't face the idea of going through that kind of heartache again.

The first train off the island was going to Stratford. A redhead who'd been standing next to Terry handed him a slip of paper before boarding it: *I want to fuck your brains out. Anne 081 488 5212.* Blake smiled, folded the note and put it in the back pocket of his sta-pres. A Tower Gateway train pulled into the station. The skinhead got on it. A woman on the other side of the carriage smiled at Terry as he sat down. Blake smiled back and simultaneously increased the volume on his Walkman. He was grooving to a bootleg copy of the Ants' Decca Demos and didn't want this pleasure interrupted.

The woman who'd smiled at Terry slipped him a piece of paper before getting off at West India Quay. This time, Blake didn't bother to read the note – he just slipped it into the back pocket of his sta-pres. Listening to Ant classics like 'Fat Fun', 'Hampstead' and 'Il Duce' had taken the skinhead back to his teenage years. As the seventies drew to a close, Terry had gone to at least four rock gigs a week. When he wasn't grooving to the bands who'd spearheaded the boot-boy revival, it was odds on he was out catching the Ants' live onslaught. Back then, Adam's mob had proved as adept at getting up trendy noses as Sham, Slaughter or Menace.

As the train pulled out of Westferry, Terry was back at the Marquee when it had been situated on Wardour Street and the Ants had a residency at the famous rock club. The grinding noise approximated the rhythms of heavy industry and sent the audience into a sexual frenzy. It only took a couple of numbers before the hacks were scuttling for the door. They went home and wrote reviews which dismissed the band as 'the fag-end of punk rock' and moaned that Adam 'mouthed the usual claptrap about dominance and submission'. As always, the trendies were totally out of touch with reality. After the Ants rocketed to stardom, the accusations of 'rockism', 'sexism' and 'fascism' were turned against the likes of The 4 Skins and The Last Resort, whose cardinal sin was appealing to a working-class audience.

'B-Side Baby' was blasting out as the train reached Tower Gateway. Terry walked to Tower Hill tube listening to 'Bathroom Function' and thinking about the time he'd followed Adam around the country on the Zerox Tour. Mostly it hadn't been a problem for the hard-core Ants' crew to blag their way into some squat. Although there was always the possibility they'd end up sleeping ten to a room in some flea-pit with shit smeared across the walls, it was a rare occasion indeed when the crew were reduced to getting their heads down on park benches. 'Rubber People' sent pulses of pleasure through Terry's brain as he boarded a Richmond train and positioned himself by the carriage door. A woman got on behind Blake and attempted to occupy the spot on which he was standing. Since the train was virtually empty, the resultant body contact was clearly intentional. As a handful of off-peak passengers were jerked westwards, the blonde contrived to rub her crotch against Terry's leg. The skinhead smiled but didn't speak. He was too busy grooving to Adam's unique brand of body odour boogie.

Blake got off at Monument and walked through the station to the Drain. A recording of 'It Doesn't Matter' from the first John Peel session was filling his lug-holes with the sorry tale of a bird who didn't wash under her arms. Outside peak hours, the Waterloo and City Line is virtually unused. The carriage Terry joined was empty until the blonde who'd followed him from the Richmond train came in and occupied an adjacent seat.

As soon as the automatic doors clanged shut, the raver who'd flopped down beside Blake put her hand on his crotch and opened his flies. Simultaneously, the Ants were joined by Jordan of Sex fame for a fabulous rendition of a sleaze anthem called 'Lou'. The blonde eased Terry's cock out of his Union Jack briefs and got on her knees before proceeding to take the throbbing love muscle in her mouth. Jordan was screaming lyrics without any regard to the damage being inflicted on her vocal chords. The raver swallowed Blake's prick and the sensation caused the boot-boy to emit a loud groan of pleasure.

The blonde contracted her throat muscles and Terry closed his eyes. The boot-boy imagined what the reaction would be if this bird was servicing him during the rush-hour. Beneath their city suits and crass moralism, Blake was certain the assembled businessmen and wimmin would find this scene a thrill. He wanted to wipe the smiles off their smug faces. As the raver pumped him up towards orgasm, he was fantasizing about boarding a peak service armed with nerve gas. Several hundred rich vermin would clutch their stomachs before keeling over to die. Terry imagined he was witnessing this spectacle through a gas mask as Jordan screamed the final syllable of her song and he shot off a wad of liquid genetics.

Blake slumped back in his seat as the blonde swallowed his come. She took the boot-boy's cock from her mouth and carefully adjusted his clothing. As soon as the train pulled in at Waterloo, the woman hauled Terry to his feet and dragged him into a rail bar where she bought two coffees. The raver quickly drained her cup, then wrote her name and number on a slip of paper, which she handed to Blake. 'Call me some time soon,' she instructed as she left.

Terry slipped her details into the back pocket of his sta-pres and then slumped forward so that his head was resting on a table. Some time later, a waitress woke him up. 'You OK?' she asked.

'You got a phone number?' Terry croaked.

'Sure,' the girl replied as she wrote her details on a pad she carried to take down orders.

Clutching this prize, Blake made his way out of the station and into Lower Marsh Street. As soon as he hit the market, Terry felt in his own element and forgot all his worries about his emotional involvement with Joyce.

As a hardened materialist, the skinhead knew the price of everything and that values were an essentialist con. When he'd lived in the Elephant and Castle, Blake had been a regular visitor to this traditional South London street market. In a nearby shop, he'd once bought a job lot of fifties' nudie playing-cards which he'd resold individually at over a thousand per cent profit! Terry scoured the area for bargains but failed to turn up much of interest. All he bought was a paperback history of the SAS and volume 18 of *The Survivalist* by Jerry Ahern.

Then Terry went into a shop stocked with a bizarre and extemely diverse range of products. The proprietor sold him an adjustable spanner and a whoopee cushion but still managed to wring change from a quid. The skinhead didn't really need the spanner but at 80p it was too cheap to pass up. Such rock-bottom prices certainly helped lift Blake's spirits. The boot-boy loved the feel of money changing hands. The fleeting contact with a trader's fingers or palm acted as a balm to his troubled mind. The kick he got from rooting out bargains was quite different from the thrills of shoplifting or rampant sex. The buzz was subtle and helped stabilize his mood. Theft and fucking were accompanied by a sharp rise in the body's adrenalin level. Since there was little

118

stress in need of discharge from the skinhead's bulk, neither of these activities would do much to improve his condition.

Next, Terry checked out the Tenison Stores. The vibrators were the cheapest in town, costing less than a tenth of what you'd pay in a sex shop. Blake already had a stock of these, which he was selling off at a handsome profit. The boot-boy bought some sticky tape and then looked at the children's toys but decided there was nothing he could do with them. The stationery wasn't much cop, not even Blake could raise a profit on out-of-date diaries. He wouldn't touch any of the biscuits or tinned food, although the governor swore it was all fit for human consumption. It was when Terry began turning over the soft-porn videos that his fingers started to tingle, a common enough symptom among hard-core shopaholics. Mixed in with all the crap, he found seven copies of Doris Wishman's *Deadly Weapons* priced up at just three quid a hit. Blake bought the lot. He knew a dozen Re/Search reading trendies who'd pay at least fifteen nicker for a copy of any video starring Chesty Morgan.

Terry didn't know that the Volkswagen pulled up on the pavement outside the shop belonged to Harold Denmark. Regardless of this, the car owner's indifference to the rights of pedestrians made the skinhead see red. Blake decided to teach the inconsiderate bastard a lesson. Using his recently purchased spanner, the boot-boy loosened every external nut on the offending VW before proceeding in a northward direction. He crossed the Thames and strolled up Villiers Street.

If Terry hadn't been a nihilist, he'd have considered the destruction of the arches beneath Charing Cross Station to be a national scandal. As well as hundreds of dossers, these had housed the best fish-and-chip shop in London and a notorious retail outlet for survivalist products called Soldier of Fortune. Urged on by these memories, Blake made his way to the Book Inn, where he bought the latest issue of a survivalist monthly which rejoiced in the same name as the defunct shop.

The skinhead cut a swath through the teeming crowds which made Leicester Square a place where the ebbs and flows of desire were palpable even to those who had no feeling for psychogeography. It was for this reason that the Jesus Army were so often to be found touting their fundamentalist message at the very centre of what reactionary wankers feared was a human flood which had broken free from the moral restraint of a repressive society. Terry was alive to the kicks to be had by any sensualist who ventured into this electrically charged atmosphere.

Despite his smart but tough appearance, Blake was not outraged by the softness of the crowd. Indeed, it was the effete quality of the masses that enabled Terry to assert his masculinity. The boot-boy was positively self-conscious of the satisfaction he gained from forcing his way through this social body. In his youth, Terry had explored the female side of his personality by losing himself within the movements of the millions who made London a world centre of sexual energy. To fully explore his Janus-faced perversity, the boot-boy now gave himself over to violating the faceless horde who swarmed out of the very bowels of the city.

The pack would run riot regardless of whether Terry gave himself up to its orgy of pleasures. It was morbid humour that led him to view this human flood as a contagion. The difference between such an attitude and the ideological orientation of a fascist was what divided order from chaos. Blake was a nihilist who sought to destroy everything, including himself, whereas the bigots of the far-Right wanted to pile corpse upon corpse as tangible proof that they'd externalized everything that was rotten inside them.

Terry delighted in negation, subversion, disorder and violence for its own sake. His badge was the black standard of anarchy. The skinhead knew he'd soon be eaten alive by the very forces he was marshalling against this world of illusion. His whole life was geared towards speeding up such a process of self-destruction. Therefore his political position was diametrically opposed to that of cultural pessimists who were attempting to slow down and even reverse what they foolishly perceived as a spiral of decline. Dogged by false consciousness, these wankers had yet to realize that death was a product of bourgeois ideology!

Most Nazis were oblivious to the fact that their influence was a million times more corrosive than that of the proletarian communities at whose feet they laid the blame for the world's natural state of disorder. As a communist militant, Blake consciously recognized his desire to surpass the destructiveness of the ruling class and systematically acted upon those impulses that drove him towards violence.

Terry cut up Wardour Street and across Shaftesbury Avenue. He hated idlers and felt no compunction about pushing them out of his way. The speed with which the boot-boy moved, provided a family of country bumpkins with several hundred hours of after-dinner conversation. It was simply one of many wondrous sights they witnessed during the course of their once-in-a-lifetime trip to the Big Smoke. It didn't occur to them that they only got away with crawling about their Shropshire farm because there was no one around to scream abuse at sluggards who fucked up the free flow of pedestrian traffic. Likewise, these hayseeds didn't have a clue about maximizing the use value of the limited shopping hours to be had in any one day. In terms of consumption they'd yet to emerge from the Dark Ages and thereby make a useful contribution to the world's growing post-industrial economy.

Blake turned right into Old Compton Street and within a few seconds had seated himself in the Café España. As a social space, the premises were essentially feminine and Terry quite consciously transformed his whole mode of being to conform with the dictates of this warm interior. The establishment served proper coffee rather than the instant muck that was so common in British caffs. The service was slow and the prices quite reasonable, which meant the boot-boy got real sitting-on-his-arse value for money. He leafed through his copy of *Soldier of Fortune* and read a report about two troop-carrying Buffels and an armoured Land-Rover which were sent into Namibia as targets to draw SWAPO freedom fighters from the surrounding bush. While Terry disagreed with the far-Right politics of most survivalists and mercenaries, he was fascinated by the machismo of this self-styled élite. The skinhead took his time reading the article and finished his coffee long before he was through with the action in South-West Africa. One of the things Blake loved about the Café España was that the owners never hassled him to get out or buy another drink. And for this alone their business merited the very highest recommendations to his friends.

'Violence is evil,' a bombed-out hippy mumbled as he stepped into Terry's path and prevented the skinhead from proceeding any further east along Old Compton Street.

'You what?' the boot-boy replied.

'You heard me,' the dirty Barbarian slurred. 'Skinheads should be put in work-camps with all the other racists and fascists. Then we could have world peace. Everyone could grow their hair and love each other.'

'I ain't fascist or racist,' Terry replied proudly. 'What I'm into comes outta black culture. Without blues there wouldn't be rock music and without rude boys there wouldn't be skins.'

'I can see you're a violent bastard,' the Neanderthal hissed.

'Fuck off!' Blake spat.

'You wanna fight?'

'Just get outta my way and piss off back to Stonehenge or wherever it is you come from,' the boot-boy said indignantly.

'Why don't you hit me? I can see that's what you wanna do. Go on, hit me!' the peace freak mewed as he formed his hand into a fist and attempted to send it cracking into the skinhead's jaw.

Terry weaved to the left and the fist glanced harmlessly over his shoulder. As his opponent stumbled forward, Blake sent a steel toe-capped DM thudding into the hippy's groin and the bastard collapsed like a bellows which had been punctured by a pin. The boot-boy ground his heel into the hippy's face, making a bloody pulp of the bastard's nose before stomping across the road. Ten seconds later he cut up Dean Street.

As Terry passed St Anne's Court he overheard two pimps squabbling over a prostitute. This immediately brought to mind an image of Joseph Goebbels and Hans Heinz Ewers fabricating the myth of 'Horst Wessel'. The latter was wasted by a fellow-ponce who didn't like the fact that Wessel had taken on one of his hookers. The Nazi propagandists transformed this petty criminal into a Brownshirt hero of mythic proportions and successfully convinced their supporters that he'd been slain by Red butchers. A rewritten version of an old German folk-song was ascribed to this beneficiary of historical revision and it soon became a Nazi battle anthem. Even today, long after the myth surrounding the ponce has been debunked, the composition is still known as the 'Horst Wessel'.

Terry cut down Carlisle Street and found himself a seat in Soho Square. The disagreement between the two pimps had set him off on a long train of thought. He was trying to remember the name of the caff he'd used back in the late seventies whenever he'd been in Soho with time on his hands. Eventually he drew the words Court Café from the furthermost depths of his cortex. It had to be ten years since he'd last been in the place. In the early eighties he'd switched to Battistas in the Charing Cross Road. He'd stuck with this joint as a West End watering-hole for absolutely ages before deciding it attracted too many tourists and moving his custom to the G & M Café in Museum Street. The Café España was simply the latest in this distinguished line.

Terry was reliving his formative years as a teenage skinhead. Quite often when there was a gig on at the Marquee, or the Hundred Club, or the Notre Dame Hall, he used to head up to the West End before lunch. He'd spent many a happy hour hanging out in Soho Market. Christ, it must have been more than a decade since the developers built a shop and office complex on the site! When Blake got bored with the Rock On record stall, he'd cruise Gerrard Street or check out the boutiques on the northern fringes of Soho. This was aeons before the advent of Mega Stores – back then Virgin was still in New Oxford Street. Blake used to head for St Anne's Court before the shops closed because he liked to thumb through the books and comics in Dark They Were and Golden Eyed. It was there that he'd bought two Crowley novels and the John Symmonds biography when he was sixteen. Unfortunately, the sci-fi specialists had closed down years ago. The shop practically belonged to his childhood, since he distinctly remembered visiting it for the first time in 1974.

Terry figured he must have begun frequenting the Court Café in 1977. In those days most of the record shops were shut by six, so Blake spent an hour drinking coffee before heading off to one of the rock clubs. Several hookers worked out of flats adjacent to the caff and they always had a rush of clients in the early evening. The time between knocking off work and returning home to their families was a convenient interlude which dirty-minded businessmen used to frequent prostitutes. Some of the tricks got so steamed up they had to stop in the caff and steady their nerves before heading back to the suburbs. The way their hands shook made them very conspicuous to any teenager with a healthy interest in sex.

Terry had never been with a prostitute. The nearest he'd come to it was a friendship with a girl who worked as a topless Go-Go dancer. Heather, the woman who'd broken his heart, had told him that if she was a bloke she'd go with a hooker. When she gave Blake the big E, she'd advised him to seek out every sexual experience he could get. 'You're still a baby,' she'd said. 'You need to sleep around more before you settle down with a beautiful older woman like me.'

'Excuse me' – the sheer persistence in the man's voice broke through Terry's thoughts – 'I see you're reading *Soldier of Fortune.*'

'So I am,' the skinhead replied as he glanced down at the magazine which lay open on his lap.

'Are you interested in guns or land-mines?'

'I might be.' The boot-boy shrugged indifferently.

'If you are, I've got a friend you ought to meet.'

'I'll wait here,' Terry hissed. 'Get him to bring the gear to me.'

'You're sharp,' the man trilled. 'If it was a cop set-up, I'd take you some place fitted out with a camera. You're a smart boy. I'll be back in five minutes.'

Blake didn't give any credence to this praise. Flattery was a sales technique he often employed himself. His pulse was pounding. If this was a genuine approach, then the seller was desperate to offload the gear. That meant the weapons were extremely hot and had probably just been used by an assassin. The skinhead worked out a bartering strategy which involved taking the dealer on to a roof at the top end of Dean Street. Having resolved this problem, Blake allowed his thoughts to wander back to the past.

The boot-boy was thinking of Jim Cross, a punk who'd hailed from Stevenage. Cross had been a UK Subs fanatic. Blake had never thought much of Charlie Harper's mob, although he'd seen them enough bloody times. Once Jim and he had attended a Subs' gig at some university in the Home Counties. They thought they'd been doing alright with a couple of birds and weren't unduly worried about having missed the last train back to London. It was only later that they discovered their pick-ups lived with parents who'd throw a wobbler if they brought strange boys home. Terry and Jim gave the ravers a quick shag in the university grounds and were left to their own devices.

Somehow they'd got inside one of the student halls of residence and locked themselves into a toilet. Blake got his head down in the bath, while Cross stretched out on the floor. About five in the morning, a student wanting a piss had tried to get in. He banged on the door and after getting no response didn't have the intelligence to go away and use a different bog. Instead, the wanker picked the fucking lock! When the door was flung open, Jim got a severe bang on the head and the undergraduate had the shock of his life. The student fled in terror after glimpsing the punk and skinhead crashed out in the loo.

'Excuse me,' said a bird with a thick foreign accent as she interrupted Terry's train of thought, 'do you know where I can meet a man friend?'

'Over there,' Blake replied, pointing at a group of youths.

'Don't you like my body?' the girl demanded as she thrust her tits at the boot-boy.

'Very nice,' the skinhead replied, 'but I'm waiting for somebody. Why don't you write out your name and telephone number and I'll call you up as soon as I've got a moment to spare.'

'OK,' the girl drawled and then wrote out her details.

Terry didn't have to wait long for the arms dealer and his mate. The boot-boy quickly sussed them as squaddies who'd ripped off some gear from their company stores. These men were anything but hardened professionals. Blake figured on buying their wares at rock-bottom prices while making them believe he was paying through the nose. In accordance with this plan, he led them into Dean Street. By ringing a trade bell they gained access to a building that had been divided into a series of over-priced office units. Terry led the way on to the roof. The squaddies followed him as he scrambled over dividing walls and across several slopes until he'd reached a position from which there was a view of both Oxford Street and Tottenham Court Road.

Terry was pleased to see the soldiers were unnerved by his antics. He'd make them wish they hadn't nicked the fucking weapons! He wanted to wind them up so much that they'd send out ripples, lowering the morale of their entire company. The boot-boy took the kitbag he was offered. Inside were six land-mines, two M 1921 Thompson Repeaters and a fistful of ammunition. Blake took out one of the guns and loaded it up. The squaddies were sweating profusely. They were convinced their potential client was a certified nutter.

Inspector James Stephens was bloody worried when he stepped out of Tottenham Court Road Police Station and headed south. The loony lefties on Hackney Council were out for his bacon. He'd been branded as a fascist pig who was unfit to hold a position of authority. Stephens was calling on all his mates in West End CID and asking them to support him as he rode out this storm. If only he hadn't made the remarks about 'tarts' and 'ethnics' in his recent charity speech! It went without saying that all his colleagues shared these sentiments but were unwilling to admit to them in public.

Terry didn't know that Inspector Stephens was in danger of losing his job. As far as the skinhead was concerned, a cop was a cop was a cop. The only thing which distinguished this officer from all the others was the fact that he'd walked into Blake's sniper sight. The boot-boy smiled as he squeezed the trigger and watched the pig collapse. The bastard was killed instantly by a bullet that lodged in his brain. Blake was tempted to turn around and shoot the two squaddies but resisted the urge.

'Two hundred,' Terry intoned.

'That stuff's worth at least two grand and we should get a hire fee, as you've just used it for a shooting!' one of the soldiers whined.

'All I did was kill a cop. What about four hundred?' the boot-boy suggested.

'No, we. . . .'

The first squaddie was cut short by his mate. 'Take it Neil, bloody take it. Let's get outta here.'

Terry took a perverse pleasure in slowly counting out the bills. The soldiers were under such a terrible strain that they found it difficult to co-ordinate their movements. Blake retained his cool until the two goons had disappeared from sight. It was only then that he gave himself up to a fit of shaking. He'd never killed anyone before! After Blake had thrown up, his sense of self-preservation returned. He collected his things together and left.

Ten

George Johnson turned his head and surveyed the assembled troops of the United Britons Party. As his supporters goose stepped into Sandringham Road they provided their Führer with a less than awe-inspiring sight. Despite the thirty-five years Johnson had dedicated to building the nationalist movement, this march had attracted less than fifty far-Right hard-liners. Worse still, the majority were cop-hating skinheads who lacked any sense of how Britain could once again become an organic community. Johnson found it difficult to hide his contempt for boneheads who insisted upon subordinating any sense of white solidarity to an irrational pride in their working-class origins.

Various shops had been boarded up in anticipation of trouble, but there had as yet been no sign of left-wing demonstrators mobilized in opposition to the cranks and crackpots whose infantile fantasies led them to believe in the existence of a master race. Johnson had mixed feelings about this situation. On the one hand, it meant that the UBP had exposed the anti-fascists as yellow cowards afraid to face the massed ranks of National Socialism in open combat; while on the other, the tinpot dictator was worried that the lack of a visible enemy might leave his troops feeling restless and disgruntled. It took violent street clashes to turn wishy-washy patriots into hard-line nationalists! And the limited skinhead support enjoyed by the UBP would be lost entirely if the boot-boys weren't treated to a riot. This march and rally had been called in support of tougher law-and-order legislation. Johnson feared he'd end up a laughing stock if his provocative political activities failed to bait the Reds into violently suppressing his right of free speech. It was very difficult to demonstrate the need for further police powers without simultaneously inciting large sections of the population to violence.

Thousands of police escorted the forty-seven UBP supporters to the east end of Sandringham Road, where a speakers' platform was hastily erected. James Morose, Johnson's lieutenant, was the first to rant and rave. When thirty-eight skinheads began to *Sieg Heil!* Morose interrupted his diatribe to berate his listeners. 'Not that, but this,' he hissed before screaming the words, 'WHITE POWER, WHITE POWER!'

Spin Harris had been bored by the whole day's proceedings and this was the last straw. He didn't give a fuck about politics and only attended UBP rallies to wind up middle-class trendies. Even to his ears the slogan 'White Power' sounded ridiculous, since the upper classes who controlled the country were Aryan to a man. The United Britons Party had failed to avail him with the promised riot, and now they even had the cheek to tell him what slogans he should mouth.

George Johnson didn't object to his followers' Germanic leanings. What pissed him off was the fact that more than half the boneheads were waving their left arms as they chanted the Aryan battle-cry. The skinheads were simply fixated with creating an antisocial image for themselves and had no feeling for the Nazi heritage whose flame Führer Johnson had struggled to keep alive. Had the UBP leader enjoyed greater popular support, he'd have indulged his inclination to punish every last bonehead who exhibited any confusion over the fact that loyal fascist cadres should only give right-handed Roman salutes.

Johnson was still foaming at the mouth as he stepped on to the platform to rouse the troops after Morose's efforts failed to meet with even lukewarm enthusiasm. At first the Führer spoke haltingly. He was looking for words to express an ideology that was too vague to be formulated in anything but the most gross of generalizations. The speech revolved around a few overworked and poorly conceptualized themes: bankers, the Jews, the conspiracy, leadership. Then, without warning, Johnson switched into a higher gear: 'Work! Honour! The Flag!' he shouted while simultaneously beating his chest.

'You what?' Terry Blake's voice boomed out of the crowd.

'Work, honour, the flag,' Johnson repeated lamely.

'What about them?' Terry called.

'As nationalists, it's our duty to sacrifice ourselves to these things,' the Führer mumbled.

'I 'aven't noticed you makin' any fuckin' sacrifices,' Spin Harris called. 'You're as bad as the bleedin' liberals, wantin' to live off the backs of the workin' class.'

Then Spin charged at the platform, and this action was immediately imitated by several of his mates who joined in as he gave Johnson a bloody good pasting. Führer George screamed in agony as the boots rained in against his prostrate body. He'd brought his arms up over his face but the steel toe-caps were still wreaking a terrible toll as they slammed into his flesh. The agony increased and Johnson found himself looking down upon his tormentors as they literally kicked shit out of his mortal shell. Grids of white light bisected Johnson's bulk. As the fascist choked on his own blood, a dark vapour obscured the bastard's view of the silver cord that connected his spirit to his body. Blood welled up through Johnson's mouth and pressure from the black cloud snapped the last few threads that bound him to this world.

Morose and the rest of the UBP leadership attempted to slip away but were prevented from doing so by the pigs. A fist tattooed with the letters HATE slammed into the lieutenant's mouth and he staggered backwards, spitting out gouts of blood and the occasional piece of broken tooth. As Morose slumped to the ground, the opening beats of the kicking he so richly deserved slammed into his bulk. All around him, other members of the UBP old guard were cowering in terror. The cops felt Johnson and his cronies had been trying to exploit the attack on Hackney Police Station and were quite happy to see them get a hiding. They had orders to protect the UBP from Reds and would have welcomed the opportunity to bash a few anti-fascist heads. However, since Führer George had failed to lay on this pleasure, they'd begun to disperse after watching his supporters beat him to a bloody pulp.

Terry Blake surveyed the havoc and revelled in a feeling of elation. Despite the efforts of middle-class lefties, most bootboys had a highly developed sense of class consciousness. Those wankers bent on creating a fascist threat for their own political ends were being defeated in their attempts to turn the skinhead movement into a modern-day version of the Hitler Youth. The likes of *Anti-Fascist Probe* were forever associating cropheads with Nazi violence, but the fact remained that the pride with which skinheads proclaimed their working-class origins went against the grain of far-Right thinking.

As Terry stood ruminating, he was grabbed by Spin Harris and hauled on to the speakers' platform. The lads wanted him to make a speech. At first Blake spoke slowly. However, as his confidence increased, a veritable torrent of words poured from his mouth. A light seemed to shine above him and there were cheers from the crowd as he announced that the working class had no country.

Anarchy! Slack! Polymorphous Perversity! Spin found it hard to make a rational assessment of what he was hearing. Could such a programme rally youngsters whose minds had been fogged with bourgeois ideology?

A fire began to burn within the hearts of the assembled boot-boys. Their grey faces were illuminated with hope. One skinhead raised the clenched fist of proletarian revolution. Another tore a Ben Sherman from his back and wiped his brow with the tough Oxford weave. Simultaneously several skins set fire to discarded Union Jacks. Hot and cold shivers ran through Spin Harris's bulk. For the first time in his life he began to sense the full potential of working-class solidarity. He watched in amazement as two of his mates jumped in the air and screamed 'Hurrah!'

As Terry spoke, he tore down veil upon veil of illusion, exposing fascism and democracy as the twin faces of capitalism. Rather than building a communitarian Utopia, these two ideologies were reducing the world to a smouldering ruin. For years a sense of anti-Bolshevik communism had lain dormant in Spin Harris's brain. Under Terry's influence it took shape and became a palpable thing.

Revolution! Revolution!

Above the ruins, Blake had dared to stand tall and raise the black flag of nihilism. A soul brother who happened to turn into the street was hoisted on to skinhead shoulders.

'Comrade!' the boot-boys cried spontaneously.

'We're all comrades,' the soul brother replied. 'We must all stand together!'

Spin Harris was overcome by emotion. Feelings that he'd suppressed for years welled up from the very depths of his bulk. An overpowering force drove him towards the speakers' platform. He stood and gazed into Terry's face. Blake wasn't your run-of-the-mill rant merchant, he was the mouthpiece of chaos itself! His eyes were bottomless pits and his brow was streaked with sweat. Terry kept stabbing the air with his clenched fists. Word upon word, sentence upon sentence, thundered from his lips like a juggernaut careering down the East India Dock Road. Harris no longer knew what he was doing, he gave himself up to the sensations of pleasure that swept his interior. 'Hurrah,' he shouted. 'The working class demands the right to shit on all the flags of all the consulates!'

Blake looked down at the boot-boy, the black pits of his eyes sucking Harris in like a welcoming cunt. In that brief moment of union, Spin was reborn. All the dross that had fogged his mind was swept away in a deluge of bodily fluids. Using narcotic endorphins as its shock-troops, the almighty DNA had seized control of Spin's bulk. At last Spin knew that his future lay beyond the gateway that had opened into the wilderness. Harris didn't need to process the meaning of the words he was hearing, he was intoxicated by the promise of freedom. 'Comrades! Anarchy! Slack! Polymorphous Perversity!' he shouted triumphantly.

And as Harris bellowed these words, he became fully conscious of how his own power flowed from the feelings of mutual self-interest that led to working-class solidarity. He had at last come to an understanding of the fact that the realization of his autonomy was to be achieved through proletarian revolt. Give it a few months and there'd be workers' councils meeting in Victoria Park! He knew now that the way forward was armed struggle against the state. This was the only means by which the masses could secure their communist victory.

'We have to get to Westminster as soon as possible!' Terry bellowed.

The skinheads marched as one body with a hundred and fifty-six regimented limbs. The seventy-eight legs that rose and fell with such co-ordinated grace had more in common with each other than the bulks to which they were attached. The boot-boys had been drilled in the school of male bonding until they'd invested their sexuality in the repetitions of the machine. The future of the fuck and the orgasm had more to do with the relentless drive of post-industrial production than old-fashioned penetration. The phalanx of boot-boys advanced upon Mare Street, where they commandeered a 106 bus.

The skinhead shock-troops made their way towards Westminster with much greater speed than the police reinforcements that had been called in from the East End to help deal with the Central London riot. The bus thundered down Whitehall and several cops found themselves spread across the road as the 106 cut a swath through their ranks. The skinheads joined the throng of anarchists and soul brothers who carved up what remained of the police line before storming into Trafalgar Square, from where the riot spread into the Charing Cross Road, along the Mall and down the Strand.

Terry headed in the opposite direction, towards the river. He wanted to find Joyce and hold her in his arms as he watched the Houses of Parliament burn to the ground. It would be hours before the cops had the area back under control. Much of the London force was still tied up in Hackney, where it had been needlessly sent to protect the UBP march. That was why Jackie and Winston had planned the Westminster riot to coincide with the fascist provocation. Rather than see ordinary people's homes trashed during street fights between fascist and anti-fascist demonstrators, the two men had decided that the class war should be taken to the very seat of bourgeois power. Khan had sent Terry to keep an eye on the UBP rally and seize any opportunity to rouse the handful of racists who gave the skinhead movement a bad name to full consciousness of their class interests. The boot-boy had achieved far greater results than anyone could have reasonably expected!

Parliament Square was a riot of colour and action. Flames were leaping from Big Ben and Westminster Abbey. The trouble had spread down Millbank and word had just reached those at the epicentre of the disturbances that the Tate Gallery had been fired. The news that billions of pounds' worth of modern art was going up in smoke brought loud cheers from the crowd. As street-hardened proletarians they understood the oppressive function of bourgeois culture. They were going to build a new world without art or any of the other élitist garbage that characterized the reigning society. It goes without saying that quick-thinking militants had wreaked similar destruction on the National Gallery, the ICA and the numerous palaces and foreign embassies located in the area liberated by the insurgents.

Terry found Joyce at the very centre of Parliament Square. She was in his arms as Big Ben crumbled and went crashing into the Thames. The comrades laughed maniacally as this symbol of imperial oppression was wiped from the face of London. To achieve freedom they had to erase, demolish and otherwise destroy the very architecture around which the bourgeoisie had engineered the domination of their class. The city would have to burn and burn and burn before this destructive frenzy reached an orgasmic resolution! Watching the Houses of Parliament

132

reduced to a smouldering ruin made Terry and Joyce feel horny as hell.

The almighty crash as the roof of Westminster Abbey caved in added urgency to their lust. A church had stood on the site since the seventh century. In the eleventh century Edward the Confessor founded the present building. Henry III began a vast programme of restructuring in 1245 and this marked the founding of the Abbey as it was known until its demolition at the hands of the feisty proletarian mob. Cloisters and monastic buildings were added in the fourteenth century, the nave and aisle being rebuilt at around the same time. Then in the sixteenth century Henry VII built the eastern chapel, which was named after him. With the exceptions of Edward V and Edward VIII every monarch since William the Conqueror had been crowned within the dusty confines of this architectural abortion. Many members of the aristocracy had been laid to rest within the building and it was good to know their bones were getting a roasting. The destruction of this ancient monument marked the end of Britain's Christian experiment and a return to the country's traditional pagan values of polymorphous perversity. And if the Royal Family wanted to stick with the religion it had foisted upon an unwilling underclass, the entire Windsor clan could go and fuck the Pope – the masses had no use for overpaid spongers whose gene pool had been poisoned from years of inbreeding.

Hand in hand, Terry and Joyce ran through Victoria Tower Gardens. On reaching the edge of the Thames they leant over the stone parapet and beneath them saw what they'd been hoping to find. Joyce jumped down into the rowing-boat, then spread her arms to catch Terry as he clambered over the wall and lowered himself into her embrace.

Terry's mouth met Joyce's lips and the girl from Seven thought heaven was in his kiss. She wondered whether the boot-boy was going to suck the soul from her body. Gradually she was lifting the veil of cynicism that had descended upon Blake, and the brand of hard loving he gave in return repaid her every effort to make him feel whole again. Joyce sincerely believed that before the two of them could settle down and raise a family, Terry had to resolve the frustrated desires of his youth. Personally, she had never adhered to the anarchist ideology of overthrowing the state – but if that was what it took to make her man happy, then she was more than prepared to erase those parts of London that serviced the governmental machine. It was for this reason that she'd helped Jackie and Winston orchestrate the Westminster riot and sent Terry off to subvert fascist youth. The way the boot-boy slid his hand under the waistband of her Levis told Joyce she'd done a great deal to help discharge the tension that had built up while the psychological conflicts of Terry's teenage years remained unresolved.

As the skinhead fingered her love button, Joyce cast off, letting the tidal flow carry them eastwards. Terry had two fingers inside the hippy's cunt as their boat drifted into the centre of the mighty Thames.

'No!' Joyce rasped as Terry slid down her bulk and began to lap at her hole. 'I wanna suck you off.'

The hippy hauled Blake to his feet and then got down on her knees. As she eased the boot-boy's cock from his flies and the love muscle began to harden in her palm, storm-clouds gathered over London. Joyce took the head of Blake's huge tool in her mouth while simultaneously working the base with her hand. She knew that for Terry speech acted as a kind of body armour and therefore wasn't surprised when he began to recite Abiezer Coppe's 'Fiery Flying Roll'.

'Thus saith the Lord,' Blake howled as though the words had welled up from his bowels, 'I inform you that I overturn, overturn, overturn.'

As Blake declaimed the anarchist classic, spots of rain began to fall on his cropped scalp. A chill wind took the warmth from the summer evening and churned the waters of the Thames. But Terry stood firm as the boat began to rock and Joyce worked his prick with her tongue.

'Behold, I the eternal God, the Lord of Hosts, am coming to Level to some purpose, to Level with a witness, to Level the Hills with the Valleys and to lay the Mountains low.'

There was a low rumble of thunder and the storm began in earnest. The rain lashed against Blake as he screamed his message of defiance to the stars. The rowing-boat was tossed mercilessly on a swell that threatened to send its two occupants plunging into the deep waters which raged around them. Joyce piled on the pressure and Terry gave himself up to terrible pleasures.

134

'For the day of the Lord of Hosts shall be upon every one that is proud and lofty, and upon every one that is lifted up, and he shall be brought low.'

For a brief moment, a flash of lightning illuminated the boot-boy, who'd thrown back his head and raised his arms to the heavens. The cops on Westminster Bridge, who constituted the thin blue line protecting South London from the ravages of proletarian insurgents, grinned wickedly when they caught a glimpse of the girl working the skinhead's love muscle with her teeth and her tongue.

'In that day a man shall cast his Idols of Silver, and Idols of Gold, to the Bats and to the Moles. For the Lord is now RISEN to shake terribly the Earth.'

The unusual atmospheric conditions sent Terry's voice thundering across London and it was heard by thousands of people. Many a wo/man trembled in fear, thinking the Final Day of Judgement had stolen unnoticed upon them.

'Remember your forerunner, who is putting down the mighty from their feats and exalting them of low degree.'

Joyce worked Terry's cock frantically with her hand. 'I want you to come,' she sobbed before putting the member back in her mouth. It was as if Blake's libido had hardened. The words of fire and steel pouring from him had replaced liquid genetics as the issue sexual stimulation brought forth from his bulk.

'Ministers, Fat Parsons, Vicars, Lecturers and Monarchs have been the chief instruments of all horrid abominations which cry for vengeance.'

Terry's back stiffened as Joyce swallowed his cock and the roaring waters sent them hurtling under Blackfriars Bridge. The rain drummed against the two figures like machine-gun bullets fired into a phalanx of troops. The very jaws of hell had opened up before them and chaos spewed forth. Blake was soaked to the skin and the wetness threatened to seep into the interior of his being. Only by concentrating all his energies on the words he was reciting could the skinhead find relief from the nausea that made his hands shake. He wouldn't allow the liquid genetics that boiled inside his groin to be discharged from his throbbing love muscle. Such a deluge would obliterate the boundaries he'd so carefully erected around the muscular structure of his bulk.

'We should be drunk every day of the week and lie with whores in the market-place and account these as better actions than taking the poor, abused, enslaved ploughman's money from him.'

The current raged around the tiny boat as it shot beneath Southwark Bridge like a bullet slicing through a storm-trooper's brain. Joyce continued to work the base of Terry's prick with her hand and its tip with her mouth. Blake's eyes radiated a brilliant blue as the liquid DNA boiled in his groin, but by sheer force of will he prevented it exploding out into this world of illusion.

'Be no longer so horridly, hellishly, impudently, arrogantly, wicked, as to judge what is sin, what not, what evil and what not, what blasphemy and what not. For thou and all thy reverend Divines, so called – who Divine for Tythes, hire and money, and serve the Lord Jesus Christ for their own bellies – are ignorant of this thing.

'Howl rich men for the miseries which are just now coming upon you, the rust of your silver is rising up in judgement against you, burning your flesh with fire.'

Joyce worked Terry's cock with an ever-growing frenzy as the boat sped through the turbulent water that coursed around London Bridge. Blake knew he couldn't hold on to his molten genetics for very much longer. His voice was hoarse and he screamed Coppe's tract as if his life depended upon his ability to complete the recitation.

'The dreadful Day of Judgement is stealing on thee, within these few hours.'

As Terry screamed these words, Joyce could feel his come spurting into her mouth. An orgasm surged through their twin bulks as the boat was swept under Tower Bridge by the raging waters of the Thames.

'And because thou hath judged me,' Terry hissed, 'I will judge thee with a witness, expect it suddenly.'

The boot-boy felt the darkness welling up around him. He had no defence against the black cloud of unconsciousness. There were no longer any distinct boundaries to mark the limits of his being. Joyce caught Terry as he collapsed.

The boat ran aground on the north bank of Greenwich Reach. The girl from Seven hoisted Blake over her shoulder and carried him back to his flat on the Samuda Estate. She stripped the tattered rags from Terry's bulk and towelled him dry before tucking the still unconscious boot-boy into bed.

Eleven

The sound of Joyce moving about the flat woke Terry from his slumbers. A dull ache numbed the boot-boy's body. Every time he opened his eyes, searing pains shot through his head. He pulled himself into a foetal position and went back to sleep.

Blake was snoring as Joyce laid the breakfast tray on the floor and climbed back into bed. She put her arms around his shoulders and shook him gently.

'What time is it?' Terry asked sleepily as he woke for the second time that morning.

'Ten past eight.'

'Time for a fuck!' the skinhead said resolutely as he tried to focus his mind on sex. He firmly believed that discipline was the surest means of discharging pain from the body.

'We'll just have breakfast,' the hippy replied. 'I've some business to attend to, I have to leave very soon. Besides, you need to recover from the wild time we had last night.'

Blake's usually unshakeable belief in the value of body culture had been broken by the excesses of the past twenty-four hours. Normally, he made a point of impressing the birds with his feats of physical endurance, but on this occasion he was glad of the excuse to take it easy. For her part, Joyce was always ready to sample the boot-boy's brand of love-making but saw his tender condition as an ideal opportunity to impress upon him that their relationship was based upon something deeper and more permanent than mere physical attraction.

'I had this fucking weird dream,' Terry said as Joyce handed him a cuppa. 'It was about the Queen dying from Aids. Afterwards, some reporter uncovered the fact that Prince Philip was impotent and so Lizzie had taken to walking the streets picking up tricks. The papers had a field-day and the British people, realizing that they'd been living a lie, transformed the country into a workers' state.'

'Sounds groovy,' Joyce replied as she gulped down tea and chomped toast.

'Yeah,' Blake laughed, 'but I'd rather smash fuck out of London than take the country peacefully. Revolution should be a continual surpassing. The proletariat needs to give vent to its blood-lust. Our liberation should be accompanied by an orgy of destruction.'

'I've gotta go,' the hippy said before throwing back the duvet and leaping from the bed.

Terry played with himself as he watched Joyce dress. As a polymorphous pervert, Blake liked to invert vanilla sexuality. Whereas dirty old men paid good money to watch birds strip, the boot-boy's depraved tastes inclined him towards the refined pleasures of observing his sexual conquests cover themselves with the trappings of post-industrial society. The way Joyce pulled on and filled out her 501s did something for Terry's soul. When the hippy kissed him goodbye, she was pleased to note he had bulges in all the right places.

Blake was fantasizing about the nubile pop singer Sinitta. He pumped up the volume and imagined that the chart-topping stunna was giving him a private rendition of 'So Macho' before the pair of them got down to some hard-core sex. As Terry came, he realized the wank had been a terrible mistake. It was accompanied by an alarming fall in the pressure which common sense dictated he maintain inside his cranium. Blake felt as if the fluids which were so essential to the smooth functioning of his brain had been sucked down his spine and were now being shot through his prick. With each spurt of DNA, there was an escalation of the agonies that racked the interior of his skull.

Terry tumbled out of bed and crawled into the living-room. A loud dose of hard rock was the only thing that would revive him. Heavy rhythms helped him to get going in the morning. He slipped a Death In June album on to his deck and, as soon as the military drum-beats of 'Knives' began to boom through the speakers, sanity returned to his befuddled brain. This live set was dated May '82, and although there was no information as to the venue at which it had been recorded, Blake presumed it was DIJ's support slot to This Heat at King's College in the Strand. He had no recollection of other Death In June concerts at that time, and what little information there was on the record sleeve did nothing to contradict this assumption.

With the notable exception of 'Nation', an incredibly power-ful instrumental, Blake considered this live recording to be far superior to the excellent studio versions the band had made of

138

these early songs. Perhaps Terry's perception was affected by his memories of the night in question, but any way you looked at it, Death In June were a band to be reckoned with. DIJ had risen like a phoenix from the ashes of Crisis, one of the best of the early hard-core punk bands. Formed in the London suburbs in 1977, Crisis underwent several personnel changes during the course of a three-year career – but the group's core had always been the song-writing team of Doug Pearce and Tony Wakeford. These two, members of the International Marxist Group and the Socialist Workers Party respectively, spread Leninist propaganda throughout the punk community.

Blake had seen Crisis perform at numerous Rock Against Racism and Right To Work benefits. The vibes were always heavy and fights among the group's fans or with British Movement fascists were a regular occurrence. Despite building up a large and loyal body of support, the band fell apart while suffering doubts over the efficacy of their Trotskyite militantism. The middle-class wankers who controlled the Leninist sects and their front organizations tended to treat genuine working-class geezers like Doug and Tony as if they were lepers. Naturally, this resulted in Pearce and Wakeford coming to question the validity of the Trotskyite cause. The disintegration of their political convictions was documented on the excellent bootleg *Red Riot Fails*, a recording of the last Crisis concert given at Surrey University on Cup Final Day, 1980.

Doug and Tony then ditched the other members of their group and recruited drummer Pat Leagas, who'd previously beaten time with Runners From 84. A year and a half later they unleashed themselves on an unsuspecting world as Death In June. Whereas Crisis had produced some of the best musical propaganda ever made to serve the Trotskyite cause, DIJ was conceived as a fearless investigation into the aesthetics of fascism. Rumours circulated to the effect that Wakeford had ingratiated himself with the Strasserite faction of the National Front. In the early days, the band opened their set with a song about the 'Night of the Long Knives', the mass arrests of 1934 which led to the elimination of the Brownshirt leadership.

'Nirvana' came next, a song which had first been performed in the months preceding the final disintegration of Crisis. Among the hard-core followers of the latter group had been a close friend of Terry's called Kate Taylor. When Blake heard Death In June were playing at King's College, he'd phoned Taylor and asked her if she wanted to attend the concert. Kate had been suffering from severe depression and DIJ's rigidly controlled onslaught snapped her frail grip on reality. During the course of the concert, she became convinced that the world was going to be destroyed on the first of June. Rather than panicking, Taylor became very serene and, at the end of the night, Terry couldn't get her to leave King's College. Eventually, they were thrown out by the security. Blake walked Taylor down to Waterloo Station. She was confused by the fact that Terry wasn't going back to Richmond with her. Kate kissed him on the cheek and then skipped merrily on to a waiting train. Months later, Blake discovered a former mental nurse had spent the next three days and nights without sleep as he sat talking Taylor through a personality crisis. Death In June affected people, and this was just one of the many examples Terry could cite.

'Heaven Street' beat its way into Blake's brain. The repetitious sound enabled him to string his ego across the muscular structure of his bulk. As he made the necessary adjustments to his body, Terry explored DIJ's mythic pronouncements on male sexuality, the occult, fascism and many other aspects of the forbidden.

While Blake accepted that some of Death In June's output appeared to be Brownshirt propaganda, he did not see this as grounds for dismissing the group's music as reactionary claptrap. Unlike Islington trendies and other *right-on* wankers, the skinhead did not feel compelled to place the Other beneath his contempt while avoiding any serious consideration of fascism as a political doctrine. Rather than responding hysterically to the merest hint of right-wing rhetoric, Terry had enough faith in his own nihilistic convictions to explore DIJ's ambiguous mythology without being seduced by it. Consequently, Blake felt nothing but contempt for those so-called critics who pointed out fascist references in Death In June lyrics but ignored the fact that a double album entitled *The World That Summer* had been named after an anti-Nazi novel.

As far as Terry was concerned, everything was fucked. As a nihilist he understood that there was no point in holding up the Strasserite programme or traditional European values as something that could save our so-called civilization from extinction. Europe and civilization were meaningless abstractions that needed to be flushed down the toilet alongside everything else which constituted the West.

As the band belted through 'Nothing Changes', Blake got his arse into gear. The necessary muscular adjustments had been made and, with his personality successfully stretched across his bulk, Terry felt ready to take on the world. Having cleaned his teeth, washed thoroughly and returned the DIJ album to its allotted place within his record rack, Blake left the flat. As he got off the Docklands Light Railway at Stratford, an attractive blonde slipped him a piece of paper on which she'd scribbled her name and telephone number. Terry stuffed the note into the back pocket of his sta-pres and then hopped on a train bound for Seven Kings.

Blake didn't mind being sent out to Essex to sign on to the Enterprise Allowance Scheme. The distance between his flat and the Beacontree Job Centre meant that the bureaucrats who operated this Mickey Mouse project wouldn't have a snowball's chance in hell of effectively monitoring his future business activities. While every EAS participant signed an agreement promising not to engage in any scam which might be construed as political, pornographic or religious, the scheme was starved of the funds with which those who oversaw it might police such a stipulation. The government would have happily underwritten the organization of paedophile rings if effective networking among kiddie sex enthusiasts brought about the tiniest reduction in the country's official level of unemployment. Anyone with half a brain could see the EAS was simply an alternative welfare scheme.

Terry was five minutes late when he arrived at the Job Centre in Green Lane. It took the bureaucrats half an hour before they got around to dealing with him and the other twenty-six recruits who'd been marshalled for psuedo-service within the capitalist economy. Theoretically, each applicant should have been dealt with on an individual basis and their business proposals carefully checked by a professional snooper. What actually happened was that they were led *en masse* into a large upstairs room where a woman read aloud that set of articles which regulated their entitlement to claim money under the auspices of the Enterprise Allowance Scheme.

Afterwards, the welfare recipients – most of whom had been coerced into drawing up plans for self-employment – were called one at a time to a huge table which dominated the room. Without stopping to read the small print, they signed the forms which transformed them into small businessmen and wimmin whose activities would be underwritten by the state. The forty pounds a week entitlement was slightly more than the money most of them had been receiving on the dole. The government considered these above-average payments well worth the extra cost, because every individual terrorized on to the Enterprise Allowance Scheme was a digit struck from the country's official register of unemployed workers.

Terry smiled at the raven-haired bird who was seated opposite him. He could tell at a glance she was shy and consequently didn't rush her into sexual negotiations. Before getting down to the nitty-gritty, Blake put the girl at ease by exchanging small talk about his business plans. The skinhead outlined the logistics of his mail-order operation but glossed over the fact that the bulk of his sales would be made up from a combination of porno videos and soiled underwear. His sparring partner was topping up her dole payments by working as a piano teacher on a cash-only basis. She was hoping to make a quick getaway from Beacontree Job Centre to give a lesson she'd pencilled in for early that afternoon.

The classical musician was writing her name and number in neat lettering when Terry was called to present himself before the bureaucrat who'd processed his EAS application. Blake stood up and simultaneously took possession of the sheet of paper the girl held out for him. As the boot-boy strode over to sign the documents that would remove him from the ranks of those who were officially unemployed, he lodged her details in the back pocket of his sta-pres. It took another twenty minutes before the last signature had been placed on the relevant dotted line and everyone was dismissed.

When Blake got to Stratford, he changed on to a North London Link train, which he rode as far as Dalston. From here, his first port of call was Ridley Road Market. The boot-boy turned over some second-hand videos and sorted through various clothes, but in the end bought nothing more exciting than very cheaply priced apples, pears and bananas. Swinging a carrier filled with this fruit, he headed for Hoxton.

Gloria Patterson couldn't believe her luck when she answered the door and saw Terry standing on the threshold of her squat. This was the bloke who'd picked her up on the tube after clocking that she was reading *The Story of O*. Gloria had taken him home and he'd actually consented to tying her up before they had sex. Unlike her comrades in the anarchist movement, the skinhead had never once suggested that her S & M deviationism was a degrading submission to the norms of a patriarchal society. After he'd left, Patterson deeply regretted the fact that she'd not begged him to give her bottom a thrashing. Now the boot-boy had returned, thereby offering her the opportunity to rectify this terrible oversight.

'Terry!' Gloria shouted jubilantly as she threw her arms around his neck. 'It's so good to see you.'

'Hi, you're . . .' Blake managed to get in before Gloria got her mouth against his lips, and the subsequent kiss prevented him from completing the sentence.

The masochist dragged Terry into the house and upstairs to her bedroom. The skinhead wasn't in the least bit freaked out when Patterson asked him to give her a beating. Blake didn't know whether she was genuinely into spanking or just testing him to see whether he suffered from any sexual hang-ups. Terry didn't care if guilt-ridden trendies denounced him as a sadist because he fulfilled Gloria's requests. It didn't put his nose out of joint if some bird got off on being humiliated.

Terry shredded Patterson's T-shirt, then instructed her to take off her monkey boots and army greens. He piled some pillows in the centre of Gloria's bed and ordered the masochist to stretch out with her stomach resting on them so that her arse stuck up in the air. Then Blake secured the girl's limbs to the bedposts. He made sure the knots were properly tightened, so that after their kinky sex session Patterson would be left with weals on her wrists and ankles. As the skinhead surveyed his handiwork, he noticed that the girl was moaning quietly. 'Shut up or I won't beat you up,' he commanded.

Gloria fell silent, but as soon as the boot-boy inserted a finger into her dripping wet cunt, she began to squirm uncontrollably.

'You like that, don't you,' Terry intoned sardonically as he worked his finger around her love hole.

'Yes,' Patterson panted.

'You'd better learn to keep still or I won't beat you up.'

The masochist was in two ninds about what she should do. She wanted to squirm with pleasure as Blake's finger worked her into a sexual frenzy. However, Patterson knew that she had to remain still if she was to persuade the skinhead to give her bottom a thrashing. In the end, Gloria gritted her teeth and buried her head in the sheets as Terry tortured her with his erotic stimulations. Tears streamed from her eyes, but this didn't matter because it was her arse and cunt that were exposed to Blake's relentless gaze.

Terry removed his finger from the fuck hole and wiped it on Patterson's thigh. Then he picked up a sneaker and tapped it against the masochist's bottom.

'Hit me, please, make me bleed!' Gloria cried, unable to contain herself.

Patterson felt in desperate need of a thrashing. It was the only thing that would remind the girl of her own physical parameters. Without the sting of a rubber-soled shoe to mark out the periphery of her being, Gloria feared she'd slip into a quagmire and be unable to differentiate her own existence from that of the great mass of humanity. Discipline and pain were the necessary building blocks of any masochist's bodily armour.

Terry raised his arm and held the sneaker above Gloria's butt for what the girl believed was an eternity. The flagellant feared she'd split in two if Blake delayed the desired slap of rubber against flesh. Realizing that Patterson was seeking far more than mere titillation from this ritual of pain, the skinhead put enough energy into the blow to leave a red weal on the masochist's voluptuous rump. Gloria felt the wind rush out of her body and wondered if she was going to collapse. She possessed a backside that was made for spanking and so the drubbing continued with a series of blows which were so savage that they made the first stroke appear as little more than a tickle. The girl became drunk with pain, but the flogging was no violation of her being. Gloria needed this humiliation in order to maintain her sense of identity.

'Put pegs on my tits,' Patterson hissed. 'There's some on the floor by my bookcase.'

'Fuck you, bitch!' Terry bellowed as he dropped the sneaker. 'What d'ya think I am, some kinda pervert?'

Then Blake picked up a tube of KY and lovingly rubbed the lubricant into Gloria's bottom. He tenderly applied this balm both to the masochist's rim of dark pleasures and the weals he'd etched into her flesh.

'Fuck me,' Patterson pleaded. 'Ram your great big cock up my arse!'

This was exactly what Terry had planned on doing and he lost no time in displaying his skills as a sexual athlete. For Patterson, this invasion of her interior was something to struggle against and thereby a means of defining her own boundaries. Everything which existed beyond the ego Gloria had strung across the muscular structure of her bulk was alien. If she could not dominate this enemy force, the masochist wanted to be enslaved by it.

'It is true', Blake thundered 'that certain living creatures, such as bees and ants, live sociably one with another and therefore some men may perhaps desire to know why mankind cannot do the same.'

'Christ,' Gloria swore to herself as she listened to Terry's diatribe, not realizing it was lifted straight from Hobbes's *Leviathan*. 'If people think I'm perverted, then they've never come across geezers like Blake.'

Terry was oblivious to Gloria's comments. He was totally engrossed in his rant: 'First, that men are continually in competition for honour and dignity and consequently amongst men there ariseth on that ground envy and hatred and finally war.'

Blake pumped up the volume and his slave greatly appreciated this increase in tempo. Gloria was moaning in ecstasy. Terry was too wrapped up with his recital from *Leviathan* to reprimand Patterson for giving expression to her feelings of pleasure.

'Amongst men, there are very many that think themselves wiser, and able to govern the public better, than the rest; and these strive to reform and innovate, one this way, another that way; and thereby bring about distraction and civil war.'

As Patterson and Blake beat out the primitive rhythm of sex, the endorphins flowed through their brains. They'd left Hoxton and their heaving bulks behind and projected themselves into other times. Terry was out on the mudflats putting down his foes in an orgy of violent destruction; living out that glorious state of nature which has been characterized as a war of all against all. For Gloria, sex was a descent into the dungeon of desire from where she came to a full appreciation of that terrible beauty which has been known since time immemorial as the Dictatorship of the DNA.

Terry and Gloria came together in a tidal wave of an orgasm which washed through their bodies like a flood of ecstasy. As they descended the steep cliffs from this peak of bodily communion, both saw the tide-mark of filth and squalor which accompanies daily life in the death factory of capitalism. Patterson and Blake understood instinctively that even their sexual pleasures were at least partially determined by the cultural norms of our filth-ridden society. If they were to build a world of ever-growing ecstasy, it would require an insurgent proletarian mass to sweep away the muck of capitalist money-making before a new life could flow through their veins.

It had not been an easy decision to make but Rupert Dawson-Rand felt he'd done the right thing. He'd seen the nuclear weapon with his own eyes and could not stand by and let Britain be destroyed simply because a lower-class lunatic was resentful about the station he'd been allotted in life. The Terry Blakes of this world had to learn that even within the revolutionary movement the duties of leadership were to be left to those who'd been bred for the task. Only the select few who'd deserted the bourgeoisie and applied to subversive ends the skills drilled into them by a public-school education were fit to hold positions of political authority.

It was common knowledge among revolutionaries that Arthur Roberts was a front man for the British security services. Rupert had approached Roberts via *Anti-Fascist Probe* and set up a meeting. Of course Arthur had denied that he worked for Seven but assured Rand he'd be able to pass any useful information on to someone who did. Having listened to Rupert's story, he warned the pro-situ not to expect the state to take any action until after the bomb had been planted. The security services would want to give Blake enough rope to hang himself. Indeed, since the nuclear warhead must have been supplied by a foreign

146

power, Seven might decide to sacrifice a medium-sized city if such a strategic loss enabled them to blow the cover of the spymasters who were behind this dastardly plot.

When Roberts warned Rand to keep his head down, he hadn't realized that this yellow coward had little need for such advice. Rupert had already organized a lengthy visit to his maternal uncle who resided in the family seat near Exeter. His relatives were pleased but puzzled by Rand's new-found enthusiasm for his roots. He'd paid them a brief visit a few days earlier on the night of the Westminster riot. Joyce had given him advance notice of the trouble because she'd assumed he'd want to participate in the uprising. While it was true that Rupert had subsequently gone around boasting to comrades that he'd been throwing petrol bombs on the front line, this tale was a lie from start to finish and bore no relation to the story he intended to peddle if legal charges were ever levelled against him. Should the rumours that he was a participant in the Westminster riot ever reach police ears, Rand had ample proof that he'd been visiting the West Country on the night in question.

Once Blake had been eliminated by agents of the British state, Rupert knew there was only one threat to the security of his position within the revolutionary movement. Although he boasted of his sexual conquests to the comrades, he was still a virgin. He found the prospect of physical intimacy with another human being somewhat repulsive but had resolved to visit a whore before heading west in his MG.

Rand drove to Paddington Station because he'd heard that hookers picked up tricks from among the thousands of sexually frustrated yokels who poured off the trains and into London. But once he reached the terminus, his spirits sank. He didn't know how to differentiate between a street-walker and the great mass of the female sex. After much thought, he concluded that the whores would stand out because, unlike genuine passengers, they wouldn't have any luggage.

'How much?' Rupert asked a bird who was standing alone.

'You what?' she replied.

'How much?' Rand repeated rather lamely.

'If you're lookin' for a hooker,' the girl hissed, 'try one of the numbers you'll find by the public telephones. I'm waiting for my boy-friend. He's six feet tall and very jealous, so if I was you, I'd piss off.'

Rupert took the girl's advice and wandered over to a phone-booth. He was bewildered by the array of cards he found. *Tall Blonde & Deadly 935 3828*; *MASSAGE 723 6291*; *NEW YOUNG MODEL KIM 224 0216*; *NEW 18 Yrs GOLDIES PRIVATE MASSAGE 486 3170*; *706 1309 Curvy-Sensuous Sexy Blonde AWAITS YOU*. Among all these messages was one card which Rand found extremely bizarre, it read simply: *SEATS RECANED 278 5647*. The pro-situ couldn't understand why someone running a furniture repair business would leave their number by a train station phone.

Even more disturbing than the means by which the crazy upholsterer touted for custom, was the proportion of cards whose designs incorporated a drawing of a whip-wielding dominatrix. Was every man in the country a raving masochist? After much hesitation, the pro-situ decided to ring the tart who advertised herself with the message *Kinky or Straight, I'm Great*. The picture to the left of this slogan was of a blonde displaying her enormous tits in a very low-cut dress. She had a sensual pout and Rupert was relieved to note that this bird wasn't tooled up with a whip. After dialling the number, Rand received directions to a bedsit in a Paddington side-street.

The pro-situ made his way up to the third floor and walked through the open door which was marked *Denise MODEL*. The woman who greeted him was not the same bird whose photogenic tits had enticed Rand to this seedy hovel. Despite this despicable fraud, Rupert held fast to his sense of purpose – he was absolutely determined to lose his virginity.

'Take your clothes off and lie face down on the bed,' Rand commanded as he shut the door.

'You said you wanted straight sex,' Denise chided. 'Kinky costs twice as much.'

'Don't worry about the money,' Rupert said as he shook with fear and excitement. 'Just do as I say.'

After the pro-situ pulled a wad of ten-pound notes from his pocket and threw them at Denise, the call-girl meekly stripped and lay down as he'd instructed. Rand could hardly believe that for a hundred quid this woman would shed her clothes as if she had no shame whatsoever. He knelt between the hooker's legs and took his cock out of his flies. Then Rupert encountered his first serious problem. He knew he was supposed to put his plonker into a hole between the woman's legs but he couldn't locate the concealed entrance.

'What the fuck do I do?' Rand sobbed in frustration.

Denise let out a short laugh. She'd taken Rupert for a heavy-duty pervert and now realized that he was actually a virgin. The harlot was smiling kindly when she turned her head and began to offer the trick encouragement.

'Don't look at me!' Rand screeched as he jumped up from the bed. The pro-situ felt as if the woman's gaze was cutting into him. He leapt backwards and went crashing through the window. Rupert experienced a brief flash of pain as his body was impaled on a set of iron railings. A split second later he was dead.

Twelve

Brighton is a holiday resort that's gone to seed. Originally a small fishing village, its proximity to London resulted in the town's rapid expansion as a brisk tourist trade developed in the middle of the eighteenth century. After George IV built a summer palace near the sea front, Brighton became a notorious centre for aristocratic debauchery. However, the toffs moved on as cheap rail excursions led to an influx of working-class Londoners.

Terry had lost count of the number of times he'd walked from the railway station, along Queen's Road and down to the sea. Back in the eighties, Blake had been in the habit of visiting the car-boot sale that was held every Sunday on a plot of land immediately behind the station. Here he'd picked up innumerable books, records and videos at rock-bottom prices. Despite its popularity, the market was knocked on the head after speculators bought up the site and proceeded to blight the area with yet another office complex.

My One Flesh had readily accepted Blake's advice that their atom bomb should be planted in Brighton. It was an ideal target with its royal palace and Victorian sea front. The warhead would be detonated right after the opening of a Tory Party conference. Republican Political Soldiers had shown the way by blowing up the Grand Hotel during a previous conservative bash. Now the pro-situationist movement would complete the job that National Revolutionaries lacked the vision to realize on a cataclysmic scale. Not only the Tories but the whole of Brighton would be wiped out.

While Terry eagerly volunteered to transport the nuclear weapon to the South Coast, he'd insisted that a member of My One Flesh accompany him on this potentially dangerous mission. As he'd explained to the Nicolson brothers, if for some reason the bomb failed to detonate, he needed a witness to vouch for the fact that he'd fulfilled his revolutionary duty.

Terry would never allow his name to be blackened by accusations of cowardice. He'd assured Raymond and Sebastian that he'd not feel the least twinge of guilt about wiping out a million or so people. However, Blake didn't expect the pro-situs to take him at his word. He wanted them to participate in this assignment so that they could witness his revolutionary fervour.

Rather than accepting this invitation, the Nicolson brothers had ordered Arnold to provide Terry with whatever assistance was required during the course of the mission. At first, Arnold had insisted that his comrades should show some solidarity and accompany him and the boot-boy to Brighton. This left the Nicolson brothers with no choice but to warn Chance that if he refused to carry out their instructions, they'd make him homeless. Raymond and Sebastian were revolutionary landlords and Arnold had never paid rent to live in the building which, according to the technicalities of bourgeois law, was the Nicolsons' private property. Therefore, Chance had no legal right to notice of eviction. Once this had been explained to Arnold, the pro-situ accepted that he'd deviated from his revolutionary principles by questioning the decisions of their collective and that such backsliding should be the subject of a future group criticism.

Having made their exit from Brighton Station, Blake and Chance cut down Trafalgar Street. Near the junction with Kensington Place, they forced their way into a derelict building. Terry took the bomb from his Ignition carrier and set the timing device. Arnold loosened a floor-board and his comrade planted the warhead in the resultant recess. When Blake told the pro-situ to hammer the plank back in place, the little shit began to shake uncontrollably and protested that the vibrations might set the bomb off. Terry could see there was no point in attempting to reason with Chance and simply performed the task himself.

'Let's hurry back to the station,' Arnold hissed.

'You're joking,' Terry spat. 'We've come down for the day. We mustn't arouse any suspicion. It'd look strange if we only spent ten minutes in town. The bomb's set to detonate in forty-eight hours, so we've got time to enjoy ourselves.'

Blake led the nervous pro-situ along to Sidney Street and into the Stage Door, which had to be one of the best caffs in Britain. The service was slow, the food was fantastic and the prices cheap, considering the size of the portions. While the walls were covered with framed posters for theatre productions, the atmosphere was anything but pretentious.

Having placed their orders, the two revolutionaries sat down at a table. Thankfully, Arnold remained silent, leaving Terry free to cogitate. Blake had been to Brighton a few times as a kid, then when he was sixteen to visit a bird who was studying English at Sussex University. The time after that had been with Heather – they'd spent most of the day on the beach. On the train back to London she'd fallen asleep with her head on his shoulder and her feet resting against a seat. Terry had woken Heather when they arrived at Victoria Station. She fell flat on her face when she tried to stand up because her legs had gone dead from being locked in a single position. Heather was embarrassed by the fact that she had to lean on Blake's shoulder to get down to the tube.

Terry's cheese omelette and chips arrived. He liberally seasoned the huge portion with brown sauce, tomato sauce, salt and vinegar, then set about demolishing his lunch. As he ate, Blake reflected on the poor standard and high cost of eating out in Britain. Thank God for the Stage Door! The guys who ran it deserved awards for their culinary efforts in the face of an indifferent nation. If anything drove Terry from London it would be the lack of decent caffs. New York appealed to his gut – the way the Americans ate put the English to shame.

Once Blake had lined his stomach, he had to wait for Arnold to finish a burger and chips. Terry eyed up the birds patronizing the caff. They were all with blokes, so he didn't really fancy his chances. This didn't worry the skinhead, since there was plenty of talent in Brighton! Besides, he fancied a spot of shopping before getting down to any bedroom athletics.

Chance became increasingly impatient as Blake dragged him into scores of second-hand shops. It took them more than two hours to travel the few hundred yards to Gardener Street. By the time they came out of the Jubilee Shopping Centre, Arnold was at the end of his tether. When Terry began turning over paperbacks on the racks outside Two Way Books, the pro-situ bolted. It was several minutes before the skinhead, who was avidly thumbing through a copy of *Small Town Sex*, noticed his companion had gone. Blake was disappointed that he wouldn't get to torture Chance with a night out at the Pink Coconut but, all things considered, the loss of the pro-situ's company was a matter of indifference to the boot-boy.

Having checked out the detective section and bought two Mickey Spillanes, Terry headed down Bond Street, skirted Old Steine and eventually found himself on the Palace Pier. He spent several minutes staring out to sea before a sudden burst of rain sent him scuttling into an amusement arcade. Blake slipped 50p into a one-armed bandit and immediately hit the jackpot.

'You're good,' a girl said admiringly.

'I'm the best,' Terry assured her as he scooped up his prize. 'Do ya wanna help me spend this? I get sick of loose change rolling around my pockets.'

Blake bought a couple of coffees. By the time they'd finished these, the rain had cleared and the two of them walked the length of the pier eating candy-floss. Having disposed of the skinhead's gambling gains on assorted amusements, the blonde took Terry back to her bedsit in Lansdowne Place.

Arthur Roberts had been pacing around Joyce as he delivered his lecture and now idled behind her as he concluded the ticking-off. As Roberts spoke, his eyes were fixed on the hippy's arse. He longed to pull down Grant's Levis and kiss every inch of her bottom.

'Look, Joyce,' Arthur pleaded in desperation, 'if I was dealing with anyone but you I'd have them locked away for treachery. Your failure to inform me that Blake is planning to detonate a nuclear weapon in Brighton is technically a capital offence. If Dawson-Rand hadn't contacted me about the plot, I might never have realized the seriousness of the case to which you'd been assigned. I'm giving you a last chance to redeem yourself. Find that bomb and find it fast. When the case is closed, I want you to retire from the service so that you can become my wife.'

'Yes, sir,' the hippy replied.

'Good.' Roberts sighed in relief. 'If you hadn't agreed to the marriage bit, I'd have had you locked up.'

The ageing spymaster was unable to contain himself any longer and let his hands roam freely over his future wife's butt. Despite her sense of revulsion, Joyce allowed the old lecher to have his grope. The hippy was able to suppress her desire to lash out because she knew this humiliation was the only way she could buy time for herself and for Terry. Of one thing Grant was certain, no matter what the cost, she was going to marry Blake and not Roberts.

'Give me a kiss and run along, dear,' Arthur trilled as he slipped his arms around the hippy's waist.

Joyce spun round and broke free of the embrace. She kissed her boss on the cheek and then left. Somehow Grant knew that, the minute she was gone, Roberts would pull out his dick and have a wank. Men were so bloody predictable!

Grant knew there was no point in combing Brighton for the warhead. Likewise, even if she located Terry, Joyce had no idea if the boot-boy would tell her where he'd planted the bomb. The only sensible course of action was to take a bus up to Graham Road, where she could hassle My One Flesh for information.

As Joyce got off the 73 at Dalston Lane, some creep handed her a piece of paper with his name and phone number written on it. She screwed up this sexual invitation and threw it in a litter-bin before scurrying down Graham Road. After much frantic knocking, Arnold answered the door. He had a blood-splattered axe in his hand.

'Christ!' Joyce swore. 'What the fuck's goin' on?'

'I killed them,' Chance moaned. 'I killed the bastards.'

The hippy pushed her way into the terrace. A trail of blood led up to the bathroom. There Joyce found the dismembered bodies of Arnold's room-mates. It took her a long time to get the story out of Chance, but when he'd finally calmed down enough to spill the beans, what he said had a certain logic to it. Basically, Arnold was mad at the rest of My One Flesh for sending him down to the South Coast to assist Blake in the extermination of the entire population of Brighton.

After planting the warhead and being dragged around a variety of second-hand shops by Terry, Chance found himself getting more and more wound up by the callous attitude of his comrades. They didn't seem to give a fuck about the millions who would die when the H-bomb went off. Arnold had slipped away from Blake while the latter was turning over some pulps. He'd headed straight back to London, arriving at Graham Road half an hour before Joyce. Having murdered Rodney, Raymond and Sebastian, Chance then proceeded to dismember their mortal remains.

'I'm not going to get moralistic about you knocking off your mates,' Joyce assured him. 'They were wankers of the first order. But don't you think you ought to do something to help the people of Brighton?'

154

'What can I do?' Arnold moaned. 'You should get on the blower to the cops and have the locals evacuated.'

'Can you imagine the panic that'll cause?' the hippy retorted.

'It was Blake's idea to plant the bomb!' Chance protested.

'Listen, I'm an explosives expert. Take me to the bomb and I'll try to defuse it.'

'You what?' the pro-situ yelped in disbelief. 'That sounds bloody dangerous.'

'I know what I'm doing,' Joyce insisted. 'You helped plant the warhead. You've a moral responsibility to do something about it.'

'Tell that to Terry Blake – he's fucking psychotic!'

'I'd make Terry lead me to the bomb if I knew where he was.'

'He's your boy-friend,' Arnold taunted.

'Shut up,' Joyce said, slapping Chance around the face, 'and lead me to the bomb.'

On the bus to London Bridge Station, Arnold apologized for his behaviour. He explained to Joyce that it had made him incredibly angry when he realized the comrades weren't treating him as an equal. However, he now understood that butchering the membership of My One Flesh was not a particularly rational response to their counter-revolutionary backsliding. Nevertheless, Chance didn't regret what he'd done. The comrades had been getting on his nerves with their superior attitudes. Arnold felt he was absolved of responsibility for their deaths on the grounds that the others had been indifferent towards the fate of humanity. Joyce, however, was quite right to insist that he lead her to the bomb. They had more than forty hours before the warhead was due to explode. The hippy could have a crack at defusing it and, if the task proved beyond her technical capabilities, there would still be time to evacuate those whose lives were endangered by fall-out from the explosion.

As Joyce got on to the Thameslink, she wondered how Winston and Jackie were getting on with their preparations to disrupt Brian Smith's midnight rally in Brixton. The hippy deeply regretted that she could not be with the boys, but duty called. Grant had to nullify the evil deeds of the man she hoped to marry. Joyce didn't pay much attention to what Arnold said as he rattled on. She was too busy willing the train to go faster.

At Gatwick, a couple of trendies seated themselves next to the hippy.

'We've just joined the Mile High Club,' the boy said, giggling at Joyce. 'We were feeling horny on the plane back from Spain, so we slipped into the toilet for a fuck.'

'Must be bloody cramped and smelly screwing in one of those chemical loos,' the hippy replied sardonically.

'At first I thought the smell was awful,' the female trendy confessed, 'but then I really got into it.'

'So now that we've figured out we're polymorphous perverts,' her boy-friend put in, 'we're looking for people who're interested in a group-sex scene.'

'Are you two lovers?' the girl trendy asked, jabbing a finger at Chance.

'No,' Joyce snapped. 'I'm a macho slut and he's a virgin.'

'That's not true!' Arnold protested. 'I'm an autosexual.'

'Sounds like a fancy name for a wanker,' the trendies replied in unison.

'Don't judge me on the basis of your repressive sexual norms!' Chance replied indignantly. 'I'm a situationist, and that means I won't fuck anyone unless my relationship with them is completely transparent.'

'Oh, I see,' the female trendy replied, 'you're into plastic! Sounds pretty kinky to me, but I don't mind wrapping myself in cling-film if that helps you get it up.'

Joyce had to admit she was amused by Arnold's embarrassment. A few hours ago he'd murdered his three closest friends and now he was being taken apart by a couple of trendies. It was the sort of incident that would only happen on the Thameslink. The Brighton service from London, Victoria carried too many tourists. Running as it did from Bedford via London to Brighton, the Thameslink tended to carry proportionately more passengers of character.

Chance breathed a visible sigh of relief when the two trendies alighted at Balcombe. Joyce always found the final leg of the journey to Brighton particularly tiresome. The train stopped to let a passenger or two get off at every hick station between Haywards Heath and the coast.

Arnold led the way out of the Brighton terminus and into Trafalgar Street. Three minutes later he was loosening a floorboard in the derelict terrace. The pro-situ used a flashlight to illuminate the recess. When Joyce saw the bomb, she broke into hysterical laughter.

'What is it?' Chance demanded as he slapped her round the face. 'What's wrong?'

The hippy tried to speak but couldn't get the words out of her mouth. Arnold slapped her repeatedly. Eventually this brought his companion to her senses.

'The timer on the bomb', Joyce explained, 'is totally fucked up. It's just a cheap watch. Terry should have used something better.'

'What are you telling me?' Arnold demanded.

'There's gonna be an atomic explosion in . . .' – Joyce used the flashlight to take a close look at the watch, hoping this would lend some credibility to her lie – '. . . four minutes and fifty-three seconds. It simply doesn't give me time to defuse the bomb.'

'Let's run!' Chance squawked.

'We haven't a hope in hell of getting out of the blast area,' Joyce replied as she pulled down her jeans. 'This is a hundred-megaton bomb. The fall-out zone will extend beyond Gatwick. We may as well stay where we are.'

'And die?' Arnold hissed in desperation.

'Fuck!' the girl announced.

Chance felt that, given the extremity of the situation, he had no choice but to sacrifice his virginity. At least he wouldn't be morbidly reviewing his life when the warhead blew him apart. He followed the hippy's lead and removed his clothes.

'Lick!' Joyce commanded as she pushed Arnold to his knees and shoved her cunt in his face.

The pro-situ didn't like the taste as the girl juiced up. This hardly mattered – he would be dead in a few minutes. Joyce lay flat on the floor and Arnold crawled on top of her. The secret agent guided him into her cunt. Long-suppressed genetic codes took control of the pro-situ's bulk and he found himself beating out the primitive rhythm of the swamps.

Joyce wasn't impressed with Arnold's sexual skills but she faked a moan just to please him. Chance had lost all sense of time. He imagined himself as the hero of a sexual marathon, but shot his load within two minutes of penetrating the girl's mystery. His prick went limp and so he withdrew from the clammy embrace of Grant's cunt. Now that it was all over, the pro-situ had mixed feelings about the business of sex. It hadn't made him feel so great, no better than wanking, and there was a lot more hassle involved.

Gradually it dawned on the pro-situ where he was and what he'd been doing. He hadn't come here for a fuck. Joyce had wanted to defuse the bomb but there hadn't been time and so now Chance was unable to explain why he was still alive.

'The bomb,' Arnold moaned. 'Why hasn't it detonated?'

'Because', the hippy explained as she dressed, 'Terry took you for a hundred thousand pounds. What you got for your money wasn't a nuclear warhead, it was a land-mine with a cheap watch glued to the side.'

Joyce felt so relieved. Her boy-friend was off the hook. Roberts could go and fuck himself as far as she was concerned. He had absolutely nothing on Blake. At the very worst, Terry could be sentenced to a couple of years for fraud, but even that was unlikely. It would be very hard to prove he'd contravened the Trades Description Act because My One Flesh had never asked him to provide a receipt for an atomic weapon.

'Are you telling me that I killed my friends needlessly?' Arnold wailed.

'Not at all,' Joyce retorted. 'You murdered them on moral grounds. That they believed themselves to be in possession of a nuclear weapon is what matters. You butchered them because of their callous attitude towards the rest of humanity. The fact that Terry conned them is neither here nor there.'

'Oh no,' Chance moaned. 'I killed my three best friends. What's going to happen to me?'

'At the very worst,' the hippy assured him, 'you'll get life. Which means eighteen years if you behave yourself. You'll be out with ten or fifteen years to spare before you collect your pension.'

'Marx, Christ and Satan!' the pro-situ croaked.

'It's not that bad,' Joyce said soothingly. 'Considering the circumstances and the fact that you've attempted to atone for what you've done, there's a possibility that you'll get away with a fifteen-year sentence. That would mean you'd only serve ten with remission.'

Arnold's life passed before his eyes. Reviewing it, he couldn't help feeling sorry for himself. Proles might claim he'd enjoyed a privileged existence but they just didn't understand! Money, family connections and a public-school education were worth less than nothing when you suffered from something like the Chance jinx. And so, for example, when Arnold offered the working-class revolutionary leadership, his kindness was rebuffed by malcontents who told him that no King's Road flake was going to order them around! All his life, Chance had been surrounded by reactionaries who would not accept the Dictatorship of the Proletariat as a central plank of the communist project!

Arnold told Joyce to get out of the building and then picked up the land-mine, which he placed against his head. The hippy scrambled into the street. Seconds later, an explosion blew out several windows, but Joyce didn't bother looking back as she marched to the station. The hippy used a pay-phone to call Roberts in London.

'Grant here, sir. The whole thing was a hoax. Blake sold My One Flesh a land-mine rather than an atom bomb.'

'Arrest the bastard,' the spymaster hissed. 'I don't care what he has or hasn't done. We need a show trial and I'm gonna see to it that he's hanged for attempting to nuke Brighton.'

The man from Seven was hopping mad. He knew Joyce didn't love him. He needed the bomb plot to railroad her into marriage. Roberts didn't care what it took, one way or another he'd make this case stick.

Thirteen

Brian Smith was seizing a unique opportunity to unite all the elements that constituted the British far-Right. It was an incredible piece of luck that Harold Denmark should die in a car crash and that only a few hours later George Johnson was murdered by his own followers. Reactionaries of every stripe were now looking for a Führer, and Smith was the man who best fitted the bill. He'd made the most of the lies *Anti-Fascist Probe* had been spreading for years by publicly announcing that behind the scenes Cockney Nation, Third Position and the United Britons Party were being directed to a single destiny by the highly secretive cadre movement known as A C Thor 33.

Smith was now claiming that Johnson and Denmark had been assassinated by communist agents. Given the extremity of the situation, A C Thor 33 and the Global Union of Fascists were directing all British patriots to rally behind the newly formed League of Racial Loyalists. With Smith as their Führer, the group's first midnight rally in Brixton was to be followed by a march through Tulse Hill and a cross-burning ceremony at a secret location.

Winston and Jackie had been working their arses off as they prepared to fight fire with fire and finally smash what remained of British fascism. To keep the cops out of Brixton, they'd been spreading rumours to the effect that they were repeating the tactics which had been used against George Johnson and the United Britons Party. The pigs took the bait and, rather than drafting men into South London, they staked out Oxford Street which they'd been misled into believing was the target of the latest working-class offensive.

Joyce resisted the urge to head for Brixton. Even if Terry was planning to pitch in with Winston and Jackie as they gave the fascists a thrashing, the chances of running into him were slim. Thousands of people would be milling around the area and, given the confusion which is an integral part of every riot, she might search for hours without finding her man. Instead, the hippy made her way to Blake's flat on the Isle of Dogs. Although Joyce had been told to arrest the skinhead for treason, she knew he was innocent and instead of obeying her orders intended to lead him to safety.

The fascists had a hard time congregating at their assembly point. They met with stiff resistance from locals who were incensed that such scum should invade South London. Bricks and bottles rained down on Nazi heads as these jackbooted morons attempted to hold their ground on the triangle of grass at the junction of Brixton Hill and Effra Road.

Winston and Jackie were holding their troops back until Smith began his speech. Hundreds of soul brothers had donned Union Jack T-shirts in a move they knew would put the fear of God into the partisans of the League of Racial Loyalists. Imagine the confusion of the average fascist once he was confronted by a multiracial army clad in what the bigots believed was their own triumphal flag!

By midnight, almost a hundred Nazis had assembled in Brixton. About the same number slunk home after being intimidated by the superior odds marshalled against them. It was already possible to state definitively that the Night Rally had been a flop. Brian Smith was only too familiar with the air of depression that hung over his followers. These men were not the best but the very worst of their kind. Unless he quickly recruited a capable lieutenant and several other officers of high calibre, his movement would die on its feet. It was with a weary heart that Smith mounted the speakers' platform. 'Work! Honour! The Flag!' he screamed.

At that moment, his audience's attention was diverted by the whooping cries of the hundreds' strong phalanx that was descending upon them. Although the Nazis were regularly given a pasting by working-class partisans, they always felt honour had been maintained if they put up a token resistance. This time the fascists just stood stoney-faced as the young rebels laid into them. Their opponents, many of whom were soul brothers, had donned Union Jack T-shirts, and that simply wasn't playing the game! Professional anti-fascists encouraged Nazis to appropriate the Union Jack as a symbol of reaction, whereas the multiracial army they now faced had effectively prevented them from tapping into the *magic power* of their standard.

Terry leapt on to the speakers' platform and grabbed Smith's collar as the would-be Führer attempted to leg it. He pinned the fascist's arms behind his back and, split seconds later, a soul brother landed a haymaker in this wanker's stomach. Smith wanted to double up in pain, but the skinhead tightened his grip and held him straight. There was the sickening crunch of splintering bone as the soul brother landed another forceful punch, this time on the fascist's mouth. Il Duce was spitting gouts of blood and the occasional piece of broken tooth while attempting to wail like a whipped dog.

Within seconds, a score of class warriors had joined Terry on the platform and were taking it in turns to literally beat shit out of Smith. As the blows rained in against the Führer's body, he lost all control over his bowel and urinary tracts. The relentless brutality of the attack caused the bastard to wince and writhe in agony. As kick followed kick and punch followed punch, Smith longed for the merciful oblivion of the grave. This really was the nameless horror – to the fascist, the assembled proletarians were a baying mob tearing into his still living flesh. As Smith's life-blood oozed from innumerable cuts, bruises and a major internal haemorrhage, a dark cloud formed within his consciousness. The light that animated the fascist's bulk dimmed and was finally snuffed out by the righteous blows of working-class militants.

Simultaneously, Smith's cadres were subjected to equally savage beatings. Among the handful of Nazis to escape death, five would die within the week, three spend months in an NHS ward and one would pass the rest of his life in a wheelchair. Fascism had been well and truly crushed! The poisonous inheritance of the Mosley years had been purged from the body politic! The insurgents would shortly consolidate their victory by imposing the Dictatorship of the Proletariat. Fascism and democracy, the twin forms adopted by capitalism according to the needs of any given epoch, would be swept once and for all from the benighted British Isles.

Following the quick dispatch of the League ‚of Racial Loyalists, rioting spread up the Brixton and Stockwell Roads. More importantly, a huge brick-throwing mob headed south towards Dulwich. They were taking the struggle into posh areas where their revolutionary violence would cause millions of pounds' worth of damage to rich people's homes. Meanwhile, other important targets further to the north were being given special treatment by a band of hand-picked partisans.

After the destruction of the Houses of Parliament, the government had requisitioned the former GLC building on the South Bank and installed itself amid the splendour of the old London Council offices. With the Metropolitan Police holed up in Oxford Street, the insurgents made the most of this opportunity to wreck what had just become the new home of the British democratic sham. Wave upon wave of Molotov cocktails rained against the edifice of the building, transforming this architectural expression of civic pride into a blazing ruin. And having successfully carried through this operation, the proletarian shock-troops headed down the road for a reckoning with Lambeth Palace.

As Terry emerged from a looted supermarket, he ran into Dirty Doug Thompson and China Doll, a couple who were friends of his from way back. Dirty Doug had earned his monicker because he got off on watching other guys fuck China Doll. After a short conversation, Blake agreed to a group-sex session in Dirty Doug's front room.

As the three insurgents made their way out of the battle zone, the majority of the jubilant British nation were glued to their TV sets. The live footage was interspersed with dismayed speeches from assorted ministers who failed miserably in their attempts to convince the public that the government was still in control of the situation.

Dirty Doug led the way into his New Cross flat. He switched on the telly as a female interviewer quizzed the Prime Minister as to why the government had not quashed the rebellion after the Westminster riot. Terry plonked himself down on the sofa and focused his attention on the angry exchange. Doug went through to the kitchen to make coffee, while China Doll unzipped Blake's flies and took his meat in her hands. The Prime Minister ineffectually claimed that no democratically elected leader was prepared to institute a reign of terror. The interviewer was subjected to a stream of abuse when she suggested that the PM was out of touch with reality.

Terry laughed maniacally as China Doll sucked his cock into her mouth. Doug came through the door and put the coffees down on a table. He whipped out his own dick and worked himself into a frenzy as he watched his girl-friend give Blake the finest head to be found in South London. There were reports that the entire population of Hackney was participating in a mass meeting which had just voted to abolish the use of money in their borough. Doug shot liquid genetics over the TV screen as the Prime Minister refused to comment on this latest development. Simultaneously, Terry fired a wad of his own love juice into China Doll's throat.

The TV was still relaying news of the previous night's rioting when Blake woke up. He'd been slumped in a chair for more than five hours and as a result his back felt pretty stiff. Terry stretched his frame, then went through to the kitchen and made himself a coffee. Having been revived by the brew, he returned to the living-room and dressed. China Doll was still crashed out on the floor and, not wanting to wake her, the skinhead left a note saying he'd be in touch.

The transport workers had failed to come out in sympathy with the rioters and so Terry was able to catch a tube at New Cross Gate. This took him to Shadwell, from where it was a further seven stops on the Light Railway to Crossharbour Station. Arthur Roberts was lurking outside Kelson House and it made his day when he clocked Blake. He'd see to it that the boot-boy was done for conspiring to nuke Brighton and that, to escape the consequences of guilt by association, Joyce became his wife!

Terry was pleased to find Joyce in his flat but his mood darkened when she spilled the beans about Roberts being out for his hide. Blake wouldn't be safe until the government fell. The riots would have to spread beyond Inner London before the politicians' grip on the nation was completely broken. In the meantime, Terry accepted the hippy's pleas that they should both leave the country. The plan they hit on was to cycle down to Welling and from there catch a train to Dover.

Terry had two bicycles. He gave Joyce the machine which was in perfect running order. The brakes didn't work on the racer Blake was riding. Roberts trailed the fugitives in his motor and cursed them when he realized they intended to go under the Greenwich Foot Tunnel. He was forced to abandon his car and proceed as a pedestrian. Terry and Joyce chained their cycles to a set of railings near the *Cutty Sark* and cut across to Goddard's Eel and Pie House.

Blake ordered cheese and onion pies with mash and parsley sauce, which they washed down with two strong teas. As they ate, Terry told Joyce that he'd long been committed to London's traditional cuisine. Goddard's not only served the best pies to be had south of the river, they did so at the keenest of prices.

Coffee gave the food time to settle. After this, Terry led Joyce to the South London Antique and Book Centre. Blake had bought innumerable second-hand Oi! records at knock-down prices in this small indoor market. He wanted a last sniff around one of his favourite haunts before he was forced out of London without any idea of when he'd be able to return. In Terry's book, no other city could act as a substitute for his home town. The boot-boy responded to London in the way a libertine might look upon a favourite lover. She was a woman from whom he could not countenance a prolonged separation.

Roberts had commandeered an unmarked car from the Greenwich police. The spymaster wondered whether he should have asked for a bike after being forced to overtake the fugitives on Grooms Hill. He parked his motor in Long Pond Road and used binoculars to follow the progress of the cyclists. Once they'd unknowingly put a considerable distance between themselves and the spymaster, Roberts slipped his clutch into gear and followed the trail they were blazing.

Every second that Joyce allowed to elapse without arresting the skinhead added to her already gross breach of discipline. It no longer mattered whether or not Blake was hell-bent on subverting the British state, Joyce was in trouble simply because she'd failed to obey the orders of a superior who wanted him brought to headquarters for questioning. Roberts was beginning to believe he could force the girl into marriage without even going to the trouble of fitting up her boyfriend.

Terry and Joyce were sweating profusely by the time they'd reached the crest of Shooters Hill. The hippy suggested they take a short break. On an impulse, they crossed the road and pushed their bikes along a nature trail. Leaning the cycles against a tree, they proceeded into a wooded area and stripped off. Terry lay down in the dirt and Joyce got on top of him. The hippy squeezed the boot-boy's plonker into an erection and then guided him into the site of her mystery. The skinhead lay very still as Joyce worked herself into a frenzy.

Roberts cursed the fugitives for taking him off the beaten track. He had no choice but to park his car and pursue them on foot. The spymaster approached the cycles cautiously but relaxed once the sound of Terry and Joyce fucking alerted him to their self-absorption. It was the first time he'd seen the hippy in her full naked glory – a wonderful sight! Roberts knelt by her bike and sniffed the saddle. The spymaster's eyes were fixed on the love action as he licked the leather that had so recently been graced by Joyce's arse.

Roberts was both aroused and outraged by the realization that the object of his affections was little better than a whore. The spymaster wanted to get his cock out and wank, but he suffered from too many sexual hang-ups to actually go with the flow of his desire. Instead, he gave expression to the anger and frustration that had been generated from a lifetime of erotic repression. Roberts took his ·45 from its shoulder holster and aimed at the hippy's head. Blood gushed from Grant's skull as the bullet sliced through her brain. The spymaster aimed a second shot at Terry but the gun jammed. Flinging the ·45 into some bushes, Roberts jumped on to the cycle whose saddle he'd been licking and pedalled off along the nature trail.

It didn't take the boot-boy long to free himself from the dead weight of his girl-friend's corpse. Anger fuelled Terry's movements as he jumped on to his own bike. By the time Roberts reached the highway, the skinhead was only ten yards behind him. However, the sharp slope of the road gave the spymaster an enormous psychological advantage. Without brakes to regulate its speed, the skinhead's cycle would career out of control if he attempted to pursue his quarry down Shooters Hill. Terry made a split-second decision – he was more than willing to die if he could take Roberts with him. In a blur of speed, the naked boot-boy rammed the spymaster's bike. The two cyclists skidded across the road and were crushed under the wheels of a Kent-bound lorry.

Terry was one of two hundred and thirty-five proletarian fatalities during a month of revolutionary violence. However, the death was recorded as a road accident and his name does not feature in histories of the period.